PRAISE FOR

The Grrl Genius Guide to Life
by Cathryn Michon

"Laugh-out-loud funny." —*Boston Herald*

"I like Cathryn Michon and her Grrl Genius related theories because she is smart, funny, kindhearted, and especially because she told me she thought I was a genius. I am trying not to be insulted by the fact that with the publication of this book, she is now extending that compliment to the entire rest of the female population."
—Merrill Markoe

"Sweet and dangerous, just like the Grrl Genius herself. Wisdom, clarity, and humor, written in the spirit of righteous postmodern feminism. Viva la Michon!"
—Margaret Cho

"The Grrl Genius philosophy saved me from 'Stepford Wife' hell. Cathryn Michon is brilliant."
—Ann Magnuson

"This book is so entertaining that when I got to page twenty-two, I felt I had to call my friend David and tell him about it. I actually read a paragraph or two out loud to make him aware of Cathryn Michon and her genius of a book."
—Carl Reiner

"Cathryn Michon puts the fun back into Feminism—not to mention the turbans, sedan chairs, and Krispy Kreme donuts. A very funny book."
—Sandra Tsing Loh, author of *A Year in Van Nuys*

"With sass and pizzazz, verve and nerve, Michon challenges us to claim respect." —*Bust* magazine

"A stroke of genius . . . think Bridget Jones in the middle of a Tony Robbins seminar. . . . A laugh-out-loud riot." —*Time Out* (New York)

"Whoever wrote the publishing rule that learning-to-love-oneself books can't be devastatingly funny didn't reckon with Cathryn Michon. . . . [She] crafts a sassy, entertaining self-help guide full of compelling autobiographical passages." —*Minneapolis Star Tribune*

"A must-have bible for women who can willingly and confidently poke fun at themselves while never losing sight of who they are and what they're capable of. Grab a Krispy Kreme and get to it!" —*Girlposse.com*

"Cathryn Michon is a genius, and the sooner you understand that, the sooner you will create perpetual economic growth, save the free world, and get laid a lot." —*Raygun*

About the Author

CATHRYN MICHON is an award-winning actress, writer, and stand-up comic. She performs in comedy clubs throughout the country, and her stand-up show *The Grrl Genius Club* is seen monthly at the Hollywood Improv. She is also one of the rare Hollywood writers to succeed in half-hour comedy (*Designing Women*) and drama (*China Beach, Sisters*). As an actress, she has worked in the theater since she was a child and has done many guest-starring television roles. She is also a playwright and the coauthor of *Jane Austen's Little Advice Book*.

Also by Cathryn Michon

Jane Austen's Little Advice Book

(With Pamela Norris)

The Grrl Genius

Guide to Life

A Twelve-Step Program on
How to Become a Grrl Genius,
According to Me!

Cathryn Michon

Perennial

An Imprint of HarperCollins*Publishers*

First Perennial edition published 2002.

Designed by Mary Austin Speaker

Illustrations by Kelly Burke

The Library of Congress has catalogued the hardcover edition as follows:

Michon, Cathryn.
    The grrl genius guide to life : a twelve-step program on how to become a grrl genius, according to me! / Cathryn Michon.
        p. cm.
    ISBN 0-06-019698-X
    1. Girls—life skills guides. 2. Girls—Conduct of a life. 3. Girls—Intelligence levels. I. Title: Twelve-step program on how to become a grrl genius, according to me!. II. Title.

HQ77 .M39 2001
305.23—dc21   2001028028

ISBN 0-06-095682-8 (pbk.)

02 03 04 05 06 ❖/RRD 10 9 8 7 6 5 4 3 2 1

This book is dedicated with love to

Pamela "Asskicker to the Stars" Norris
(GRRL GENIUS)

The Twelve Steps
of the Grrl Genius Program

Step One: We Admitted That We Were Grrl Geniuses

Step Two: Were Entirely Ready to Embrace the Domestic Arts

Step Three: Boldly Accepted Our Grrl Genius Mortality

Step Four: We Commited Ourselves to Our Grrl Genius Relationship (or Didn't)

Step Five: Came to Believe That a Grrl Genius Works Well with Others

Step Six: Made a Decision to Love Our Grrl Genius Good Looks

Step Seven: Made a Searching and Fearless Inventory of Our Sexuality and Embraced It!

Step Eight: Sought to Reject Penis Envy

Step Nine: Came to Believe in a Grrl Genius Higher Power Greater Than Ourselves

Step Ten: Continued to Celebrate the Grrl Genius Aging Process

Step Eleven: Were Entirely Ready to Love the First Grrl Genius We Ever Met, Our Mother

Step Twelve: Having Had a Grrl Genius Awakening, We Carried the Message to Others by Practicing These Principles in All Our Affairs

Contents

GRRL GENIUS APPENDICES

Delusions of grandeur make me feel a
lot better about myself.

—LILY TOMLIN
(Grrl Genius)

We are what we think, all that we are arises with our
thoughts. With our thoughts we make the world.

—BUDDHA
(Enlightened Male)

Step One

"We Admitted That We Were Grrl Geniuses"

It takes a lot of time to be a genius, you have
to sit around so much doing nothing,
really doing nothing.

—GERTRUDE STEIN

I know all the people worth knowing
in America, and I find no intellect
comparable to my own.

—MARGARET FULLER

The Grrl Genius Guide to Life is a twelve-step program that will show you how to become a Grrl Genius, according to me, Cathryn Michon, Grrl Genius.

Oh yes, make no mistake, I am a Grrl Genius, and you can be one too. All you have to do is take the first step. All you have to do is admit that you are a genius. Also you must be willing to acknowledge the genius of any other Grrl who takes the leap of faith and admits her genius.

I took the "Great Grrl Genius Leap Forward" and proclaimed myself a Grrl Genius based on no actual evidence whatsoever. I discovered that I was a genius because I said I was! Truly it was as simple as that, and my life has changed dramatically for the better since I took this simple, seemingly bizarre first step.

Why did I take this radical action? Because I simply woke up one morning and realized that I was sick to death of feeling like a fat, wheezing pig and a loser for many, if not all, twenty-four hours of the day. I knew logically that I was neither a loser nor fat and wheezing. Still, my first thought on waking up was usually that I was ten years and $10,000 behind. I never felt pretty enough, good enough, talented enough, or smart enough.

I thought that part of the reason for this might be because I live in Los Angeles. For one thing, Los Angeles is the global epicenter of female-body loathing. In this gleaming metropolis, through the media of television, film, and popular music, billions of dollars are made exporting revulsion for the natural female form throughout the known world.

It seems that every woman in L.A. has been surgically altered. In Los Angeles, the ideal woman is a modern Minotaur, a mythical creature whose bottom half is from a completely different species than her top half. If you're the ideal L.A. woman, you're concentration-camp-victim thin on the bottom, but on the top you're supposed to have two happy, shiny beach balls of pleasure and joy. On the bottom you're supposed to be so thin that you can no longer menstruate or bear live young or have an opinion of any kind. On the top you're supposed to be able to lactate enough milk to fill all the latte orders at your local Starbucks.

This is completely unacceptable.

As a Grrl Genius, I feel it is my duty to point out that no woman exists in nature who has the ass of a seventeen-year-old boy and the udders of a Guernsey cow. It just doesn't happen.

Then I realized it wasn't just living in L.A. that was giving me terminally low self-esteem. Apparently women all over America have been feeling like fat, wheezing pigs and losers. In a recent *People* magazine poll, 91 percent of women said they were "dissatisfied" with the way they look. I was sick of being depressed because I could never live up to the impossible ideals that assaulted me on television and in movies and magazines. My career was no compensation for this gnawing feeling of inadequacy. I liked my career okay, but I felt I was nowhere near as successful as the men I worked with.

I wanted to blame men or the media or society, but that always makes me crabby, and I was sick of doing it. Then, I had a life-altering revelation. This was the revelation that started me on my personal "Journey to Genius." The sky opened up and a giant beam of golden light enveloped me, and a deep, mellifluous voice that sounded very much like Maya Angelou's began to speak to me—

Okay, that's not what happened. My giant revelation came as I was naked, eating Häagen-Dazs Dulce de Leche ice cream, drizzled with hot fudge and caramel sauce and covered in slivered pecans. It's the most incredible, delectable dessert. It's a magnificent combination of pecan pie and ice cream and chocolate turtles, all in one, as well as being a delightful and disease-free substitute for sexual activities of all kinds.

By the way, I invented that dessert, which really ought to be proof enough of my genius for any of you who are doubting me so far. Please see the "Grrl Genius Appendix" for the (brilliantly simple) recipe.

The life-altering revelation I had while eating that fantastic dessert was that it wasn't men or the media or anybody else who had the final say on whether I was pretty enough, good enough, talented enough, or smart enough. I realized, as I sat in my kitchen, warm golden droplets of caramel sauce occasionally dribbling onto my breasts, that I was, in fact, the boss of me. Sure, maybe it was the sugar talking, but the revelation itself was very real. For maybe the first time in my life, I actually understood that I was, in fact, the only person in the world who could decide how great I was or wasn't.

So I decided to be a genius. A beautiful, talented Grrl Genius.

The first person I "came out" to about my genius was my friend Wendy, a brilliant writer and actress. We were talking about how difficult it was to get show business jobs because of the "old boys' club." I came up with the plan to form a "Grrl Genius Club," and so we agreed to start calling each other geniuses, based on no empirical evidence whatsoever. The only rule of our club was that we had to, at all times, refer to ourselves, and every other woman we liked, as geniuses, even if it seemed weird. If anyone ever mentioned Wendy's name, especially in a work situation, I had to proclaim in a loud, confident voice:

"Wendy Goldman? Oh my God, she's such a genius, you know that, right?" And of course, she is.

Wendy agreed to do the same for me, and that's how the (soon-to-be) worldwide Grrl Genius craze began. I then told my friend Diane Driscoll (Grrl Genius), and then she started telling other girlfriends, and they told their girlfriends, and everyone really liked the idea, and why shouldn't they? Who doesn't like being called a genius?

And then I developed my twelve-step program. The first step of which is:

"Admitted that we were Grrl Geniuses."

Men, in addition to having scrumptious broad shoulders and adorably knobby knees, know how to proclaim their genius, and other men's genius as well; it's one of the best things about them. In one week alone, I heard men say the following:

"I like to fart in public, that's just part of my genius."

"Jim Varney was a comic genius."

"I'm a genius at making grilled cheese."

When asked about their own gifts, most women will say, "I'm okay, I'm pretty good." If asked about another woman, they will usually say something like, "I think she's talented, I mean, I like her, you might not, but she's really pretty good."

If asked whether she can make a grilled-cheese sandwich, a woman is likely to say, "Yeah, I can make a grilled-cheese sandwich, who the hell can't? Now do you want one or not, because I haven't got all day! And please stop farting."

Women also never proclaim themselves geniuses of grilled cheese or anything else, even if they are, because they don't want to seem stuck-up.

Until now.

Until the launch of my (impending) Grrl Genius worldwide campaign for world peace, economic prosperity, sexual fulfillment, and all-around fun increasement, Grrls were too shy, too beaten down by themselves, to recognize and celebrate their inherent Grrl Genius. The sooner Grrls everywhere begin to proclaim their genius, the sooner we will all enjoy the benefits of the (very imminent) Grrl Genius Revolution.

This is not a joke.

You may be on board with the whole "Genius" concept but somewhat unsure of the "Grrl" part. *Woman* is a perfectly fine word, but frankly, I think it's got a lot of tough memories attached to it. "Women's suffrage," "Women's oppression," "battered Women." These are not cheerful phrases. It's not the word's fault, it's just the way things have been.

But not anymore.

Grrl isn't associated with anything bad from the past. *Grrl* is just breezier, less loaded, its two *r*'s give it a fun edge and let you know that a Grrl is tough and sassy and fun and smart and proud.

What about the men? How do they fit into this brave new Grrl Genius world? Men are more than welcome in the Grrl Genius Club, all they need to do is acknowledge the genius of Grrls in general, and the Grrls they know in particular. If they acknowledge this genius, then they become "Enlightened Males" and automatic members of the Grrl Genius Club. Plus they will find that they tend to get more frequent and higher-quality sex. Don't ask me why, that's just how it seems to work.

So Enlightened Males must say that Grrls are geniuses, but do they have to mean it? Absolutely not. Enlightened Males can be as insincere as they like when they call us geniuses; after all, we don't necessarily mean it when we call them geniuses either. All we are looking for is a little mutual insincerity.

Rest assured that working the Grrl Genius twelve-step program is not about hating men, far from it. In fact, you will notice that throughout the book, almost every time I mention men's genitalia, I speak of them only in the most laudatory of terms. Terms like "his turgid love ingot" or "his engorged scepter of lust." There are a few reasons for this:

A. I like men and their genitalia.

B. I once spent an entire extended, expensive vacation reading Harlequin romances, then inventing various exotic and thrilling terms for the male member as "research" for a screenplay I was going to write.

C. I never actually wrote the screenplay, but if I use the terms in this book, well, let's just say that it could be helpful "tax-wise."

By the way, I'm not the only author to make textual choices for tax reasons. It's a little-known fact that the working title for Peter Mayle's wildly successful *A Year in Provence* was *How Am I Gonna Write Off This Big Expensive French Country House?* It's a little-known fact, because I made it up.

I hope the reader will indulge my literary tax planning. A Grrl Genius has to make her money stretch as far as it can. After all, I have a mentally ill cat, a medicated Doberman, and a diabetic cat named Kandy (don't ask) to look after.

That's just part of my genius.

When I began to develop the twelve steps of the Grrl Genius program, I started doing research on how the whole notion of Grrl Genius had fallen into such a state of worldwide disrepute. I started wondering why no one, at that time, ever seemed to call women geniuses. I thought to myself:

"Why is Frank Sinatra a genius and Ella Fitzgerald just a girl with a good set of pipes?

"Why is Wolfgang Puck a genius and Julia Child just a nice lady with a lot of cookbooks?

"Why is Henry Kissinger a genius and Madeleine Albright just a tough broad with a lot of frequent-flier miles?"

For the answers to these and other questions, I went to the enormous Forty-second Street branch of the New York Public Library. Under the subject heading "genius," there were 203 books, none of which were about women. They included titles like *The Man of Genius, Average Man Against Superior Man, The Sons of Glory: A Study of Genius, A Study of Greatness in Men, General Types of Superior Men,* etc. ad nauseam.

When I did an individual word search to try to find anything about women's genius, I came up with discouraging titles like *Wives of Men of Genius* and the particularly upsetting *Almost a Man of Genius.*

I started to get very cranky, suicidally cranky. I found that, due to some poor planning by the architect, there is no convenient, private place to slit your wrists at the New York Public Library and no large balcony from which to hurl yourself. So I continued my search. What I found was that of the 203 books about men and their genius, only six of them were written by women, and even those six women chose to write only about men.

This is intolerable.

I then decided to do some research on the word *genius* itself. The word derives from Latin and refers to the goddess Juno, the Roman queen of heaven, which was a fantastic job title, because apparently she was pretty much the boss of everyone. The Romans believed that every person carried within himself or herself a small version of this goddess, a sort of geniusette, who would inspire each to greatness. So, in fact, the word *genius* means literally "the goddess within," or more colloquially, "Grrl Genius."

The word *genius* actually means "Grrl Genius"!

Therefore, when we call each other Grrl Genius, we are actually being slightly redundant, because we are literally calling each other "Grrl Grrl Geniuses." However, until the (forthcoming) global tide of Grrl Genius crests, we will simply have to put up with such minor linguistic snafus.

The other interesting thing about the goddess Juno was that she could have babies by herself, if she wanted to, or she could have lustful relationships with gods or men. So she went back and forth from being a chaste virgin to a deity of sexual lust.

Like who doesn't?

I believe that over three thousand years of undervaluing Grrl Genius has left a legacy of war, genocide, famine, pollution, and violence. I know that sounds bad, and of course it is. However, I believe that the (soon-to-be) Grrl Genius phenomenon will bring humankind further and further away from these useless and annoying activities.

I recommend that you take at least thirty days to complete your own "Journey to Genius." You will notice, as you work your way through the twelve steps, that I have illustrated each of these concepts with not particularly flattering but true stories from my own life. You may find yourself saying, "The things Cathryn is telling me about don't seem geniusy at all; in fact, they seem really embarrassing and moronic."

That is exactly the point.

Being a Grrl Genius is not about being perfect. That's why this is a very "doable" program. Even as the word *genius* has traditionally been applied to men, the embarrassing quirks and foibles of geniuses always served merely as further proof of true genius. Nobody remembers Einstein for having wretched personal hygiene or for being behind on his rent from time to time (both of which are true, by the way). They remember him as a genius.

You can make this same sort of denial work for you. For example, if you are behind on your bills, you may be thought of as a slacker or a deadbeat. If you are behind on your bills once you declare yourself a Grrl Genius, the implication is that you have important, geniusy reasons for being broke. As a genius, you are probably too busy thinking big thoughts to be concerned with the mundane realities of life.

Since I became a Grrl Genius, nearly all my character

flaws have mutated into charming evidence of my brilliance. My insistence on beautiful but impractical footwear, my inability to balance a checkbook, my fear of clowns, all of these formerly annoying traits are now just part of my genius.

Every woman on earth is potentially a Grrl Genius. In working the twelve steps of the program, you will discover that certain patterns of behavior are more conducive to your genius than others. These distinctions are subtle and will become apparent over time.

Interspersed throughout the chapters covering the twelve steps, you will find "Grrl Genius Little Pink Post-its." These are little notes I wrote to myself on little pink Post-its as I braved my way through the twelve steps for the first time. Mostly, they are true and inspiring facts about the history of Grrl Geniuses that will give you strength to keep to the "Path of Genius."

You will also find recipes, lists, quizzes, Grrl Genius quotes, and even a lovely craft project to help guide you along your way.

The Grrl Genius program, like other twelve-step programs, has slogans, little sayings, and aphorisms that you can cling to in rough times. They are a shorthand version of the program, to remind you of your genius whenever you need it.

The Slogans of the Grrl Genius Guide to Life
Twelve-Step Program

Today Is the First Day of the Rest of My Genius

Success Is Ten Percent Inspiration and Ninety Percent Self-Delusion

Don't Quit Before the Miracle Happens—to Someone Untalented

Let Go and Let Genius

Let There Be Genius on Earth and Let It Begin with Me

Denial, It's a Good Thing

Keep It Simple (and Elegant)

If You're Not Part of the Solution, You're Very Annoying

There's Nothing Wrong With My Butt

One Grrl Genius Day at a Time

Skeptics could look at the Grrl Genius program and say to themselves, "This whole thing is nothing but a load of self-delusional brainwashing."

They would be right.

Self-delusion is one of the most powerful tools on earth. Napoleon was deluded with the idea of being the emperor of France, and then he became—here's what—the emperor of France. A Sri Lankan fire-walker deludes himself into thinking he can walk barefoot on hot coals, and then happily tiptoes across a barbecue. Jane Austen believed, despite the discouragement of everyone around her, that a woman could write a novel, and she became perhaps the most widely read novelist in English literature.

All great achievements begin with delusions of grandeur. The power of self-delusion has even been documented by scientists. In controlled experiments, people who pretended to have high self-esteem actually started to feel better about themselves and achieved more. Reality is clearly an overrated concept.

Now it is time for you to take that all-important first step: "Admitted that we were Grrl Geniuses."

Just click your heels together and say three times, "I am a Grrl Genius." I'm serious. I did it. I do it all the time. I'm not even lying. I do the heel clicking and the whole deal. For real.

Come on, just do it. If people can see you, go where they can't and just do it.

I know it seems silly, and the heel clicking is a blatant rip-off from the *Wizard of Oz*. But the Virgin Birth was a blatant rip-off of the Shiva cult of Hinduism, and yet that hasn't stopped thousands of people from being miraculously cured by visions of Mary found on tortillas, has it? Mysteries of faith are not quantifiable, but you can't partake of these mysteries if you don't at least try.

Just do it, just admit you are a genius. After all, what do you have to lose except your chronic, terminal low self-esteem? In the immortal words of Grrl Genius Eleanor Roosevelt:

"No one can make you feel inferior without your consent."

And no one will ever call you a genius if you don't do it first. So just click your heels and say it:

"I am a Grrl Genius, I am a Grrl Genius, I am a Grrl Genius."

I promise you, your life will never be the same.

A Special Note to

THE ENLIGHTENED MALE

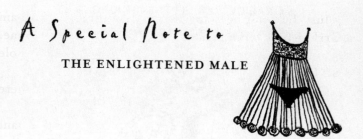

If you have a tumid, yearning ardor ingot, or a manly shaft of eager desire, and you're reading this, you are an Enlightened Male.

I'm not saying that just to pucker my full, red lips and blow a lot of hot air into your ear, although I know how much you like that.

Any man who would read this book, this far, is a living, breathing example of a great evolutionary leap forward, the best hope for peace on earth and economic plenty for all, and obviously dynamite in the sack.

That isn't idle flattery. Oh, it's flattery all right, it's just not idle.

Join me in my secret garden of Grrl Genius. It's so obvious that you're not threatened by brilliant women, and why should you be? As brilliant as you are, you don't need to make others seem small just so you can feel big.

You're big already.

You'll probably get a big kick out of this book, it's chock-full of good information you surely already know. Maybe you could pick up a few pointers—as an Enlightened Male, you're always looking to better your game, aren't you?

Hopefully you'll be amused, and a little more enlightened when you're through.

Plus, all that extra, high-octane sex.

Welcome!

A GRRL GENIUS LITTLE PINK POST-IT

Hey, Grrl Genius!

Whenever people need an example of a genius, they usually pick Einstein, as in "He's no Einstein."

The Einstein to whom they are referring is, of course, Man of the Century and noted bad dresser Albert Einstein, but they might as well be referring to Mileva Maric Einstein, Albert's first wife. Mileva and Albert were both physics students when they met, although she got better grades than he did and was considered to be a superior mathematician. In addition, she was considered a much snappier dresser and a more frequent bather as well.

What few people know is that Albert and Mileva actually coauthored the paper in which the $E = MC^2$ equation was first discussed, as well as two other early significant papers. As his notoriety grew, Albert had his wife's name removed from the papers in subsequent publications. Einstein himself is quoted by his son and a student who lived with them as having said that Mileva "solved all my mathematical problems." "Doing the math" in physics is not incidental; "doing the math" in physics is like "taking off the clothes" in stripping—it's everything.

Certainly Einstein scholars have downplayed the role

that Mrs. Einstein played in the revolutionary theories of her husband, Albert. Mileva Maric Einstein was obviously an uncredited Grrl Genius who never fully explored her own potential, weighed down as she was with the care of two sons, one of whom was mentally ill.

I'm sure there are those who would scoff at the idea of Einstein having any weakness as a mathematician. To those skeptics, I would say that Einstein's mathematical weakness is evidenced not just in lower scholastic grades, but also in the fact that he was known to be incapable of remembering his wife's birthday, a simple sequence of four digits.

A GRRL GENIUS LITTLE PINK POST-IT

Hey, Grrl Genius!

Another person whose name has become synonymous with the word *genius* is Wolfgang Amadeus Mozart. There is another, lesser-known Mozart, however, Wolfgang's Grrl Genius sister Nannerl, who was also a child prodigy. Although this is usually omitted from the Mozart story, brother and sister traveled throughout Europe together with their father to all the fancy-pants courts and castles of Europe, where they performed for royalty, who wouldn't know a good song if it bit their crown off.

At fifteen, Nannerl, who had been Wolfgang's only companion, was sent home to be married off. Many musicologists have speculated that compositions attributed to Wolfgang may actually have been written by Nannerl.

The same people who blame Yoko for breaking up the Beatles would probably ridicule the idea of Mozart's sister having been a Grrl Genius composer. It's important to note that Mozart himself is quoted in his letters as saying that he considered his sister to be "the talented one."

The controversy over who composed the symphonies

will probably never truly be settled. What remains undisputed is the simple fact that nobody could come up with a better fart joke than one Mr. Wolfgang Amadeus Mozart. When it came to putting a whoopee cushion under a royal ass, nobody did it better than "Wolfie."

Step Two

"We're Entirely Ready to Embrace the Domestic Arts"

You can't be spoiled if you do your own ironing.

—Meryl Streep

I was going to commit suicide by sticking my head in the oven, but there was a cake in it.

—Lesley Boone

Before I became a Grrl Genius, I struggled for years with the political question of who should bring home the bacon, and who should fry it up in a pan, and furthermore, what about those pesky nitrates? I mistakenly thought that to be a Grrl Genius I had to eschew all the domestic arts, but then I discovered that as a true Grrl Genius, I could have my cake and eat it too! (Although I have never understood that cliché; of course if you have cake, you should eat it, what else are you going to do with it, wear it on your head? Besides, it's physically impossible both to have cake and eat it too, because once you eat the cake, you no longer have it. You have to accept that you can either have cake or eat it, and obviously eating it is the best choice. Unless you have a whole package of, say, six Little Debbie snack cakes, in which case you can both have cake, in the form of five uneaten Little Debbies, and eat it too, in the form of the one Little Debbie you are currently eating.)

Anyway, cake aside, the point is I realized that cooking can be a Grrl Genius activity, once I emphatically declare that it is! And it's even more geniusy if I cook competitively, so that's why I now enter cooking contests of all kinds. That is how I used my genius to make peace with the domestic arts—I turned it into a contest, and you should too!

As a result of my competitive cooking frenzy, I am here to report that for the fourth year in a row I have come in third at the "Live Salad-Making Competition" at the Santa Barbara County Fair. Once again I'm bringing home the bronze. It's like I've become the Lu Chen of salads. You remember Lu Chen, the brilliant Chinese skater Grrl who always got third at the Olympics, even though she was better than everybody else. Even though she never got involved in any of those embarrassing knee-whacking, bridal-porn, drunk-driving, or swearing-at-Mickey-Mouse skater-Grrl scandals. Lu Chen always gets passed over, and so do I, and I'll tell you this much, we're both sick to death of it.

Actually, the whole live salad-making frenzy started when my friend Pam, a brilliant Grrl Genius comedy writer, suggested that a bunch of us who were frustrated in our showbiz aspirations should enter the county fair in cooking competitions. Because at least the salads, unlike movies and television shows that live in our heads, would get made.

Now I find, after four long years, that I am as bitter about the whole world of live salad-making as I am about show business. Live salad-making is *very* political, it's all about who you know.

I'll never forget the first year of competition, my salad days, if you will. By the way, I should mention that in the first year, my husband, who had never baked a pie before and really hasn't made one since, not only won first place for his "Brazilian Lime Pie," he won Best of Show for the whole fair. It turns out, he's some kind of idiot savant of pastry. Who knew?

Anyway, the first year I made "Cathryn's Grrl Genius Low-Fat Technicolor Tater Salad." (Please see "Grrl Genius Appendix" for the recipe for this salad.) It's made with red potatoes, white potatoes, yellow potatoes, and purple potatoes, and it is a sight to behold. And it wasn't just a salad; I felt it was a witty commentary on the artificiality of the American Dream. As I prepared it live onstage, I wore a tiara with small new potatoes on it, which I insisted on calling my "pomme de tiara," not that any of those plebeian, lowbrow, hack judges got any of it.

My friend Pam wore all black with a tasteful necklace of pearl onions. Classy, smart. Her salad was all about the false comfort of the bourgeoisie. Her salad was entitled "The 1980 Wretched Excess Retro Surf-and-Turf Salad." It took $97 worth of ingredients to make, including lobster, steak, caviar, and deviled eggs, and it basically amounted to nothing so much as a bribe on a plate. And it was a bribe those judges were happy to take, because they gave her second place, although they completely missed the tongue-in-cheek social irony of both our salads. They just ate them; they just thought they were "good salads."

This is where the story gets really sad and bitter, like so many of my stories. My Grrl Genius friend Cassandra was also in the contest. Now, Cassandra actually wore a full sari, complete with third-eye dot, and it was obvious to all discerning salad-eaters that she clearly deserved to win first prize with her "Indian Monsoon Masala Salad," a wry homage to the spirituality of India. But she got completely hosed: she didn't even place! And you know why? Because her salad was just too goddamned hip for the room, that's why.

I know, because after the competition I confronted one of the judges, a certain Mrs. Peggy Keefer. Yes, the very same Mrs. Peggy Keefer who was the previous year's winner because she supposedly makes her own balsamic vinegar. Ha! I for one would like to see the still.

Anyway, I confronted Peggy Keefer after the competition. I wanted to know why Cassandra's obvious vegetarian excellence was so egregiously overlooked, and here's what Mrs. Peggy Keefer had to say about Cassandra's salad: "Well, I liked it, but it had too many flavors." Too many flavors! Too many flavors for the simpleminded palate of Mrs. Peggy Keefer!

By the way, we took a video of that first competition, and I will endeavor here on paper to describe the images captured on that video. I will give you an instant replay, as it were, of what I did onstage after they did not award Cassandra first place. I said (jaw drops, screaming), "Nooooooo!" Just as everyone has ever wanted to do at the

Oscars. If I had been at the Oscars, I'd have been screaming, "Marisa Tomei? Noooooooo!"

I was that stunned.

Of course, it should come as a surprise to no one that
the woman who won first place just happened to be friends
with—yes, you guessed it—a certain judge named Mrs. Peggy
Keefer. This "friend" of hers showed up with her "salad,"
a pathetic combination of grilled roadkill, with hideous
wilted spinach and pine nuts.

Oh, wait a minute, now it's all making sense! Pine nuts,
that must be the secret, why didn't we think of pine nuts! It
wasn't her obvious, sycophantic, ass-kissing friendship with
a certain Mrs. Peggy Keefer. It was the goddamn pine nuts!

Mrs. Peggy Keefer. The supposed vanguard of salads. I
mean, can we just all agree, how *over* is balsamic vinegar?
What other saladic innovations does she have up her soiled
polyester sleeve? Please, I suppose she's busy growing her
own iceberg lettuce too. Perhaps next year she will treat us
to homemade "Bac*Os" or some of her "Creamy Ranch
Dressing" that's all the rage in whatever fetid trailer park
she currently calls home. That's how behind the salad curve
a certain Judge Mrs. Peggy Keefer is.

So anyway, this year, the theme of the fair was "California Diversity," a theme I embraced by wearing my trademark tiara covered with the flags of the nations of all our
Pacific Rim neighbors. I made "Cathryn's Grrl Genius
Can't We All Get Along Salad,"subtly invoking the plaintive appeal of a certain Mr. Rodney King. It was made
entirely of vegetables that represent all of our beautiful cultures in the melting pot—or in this case, the cold platter—
that is California. It was cleverly molded into the shape of
our fair state, complete with California strawberries out-
lining the San Andreas Fault. Surrounding all this was the
word *California,* lovingly spelled out in red, white, brown,

and yellow roasted peppers, which represented our unique panorama of multicultural skin tones, each special, and tasty, in its own way. As always, there was a message in my roughage.

But still I'm third. And who won? The astute reader will see this coming: yes, a certain Mrs. Peggy Keefer's new pet, Michelle Nassberg. And what did she make? Certainly the prize winning salad must have been exotic beyond our wildest fancies, right?

Guess again. She made just a plain old tossed salad. Yes, you heard me correctly, a sad and greasy tossed god-damned salad, with shaved carrots, just like you get on your tossed salad from, oh, let's say Burger King. But of course her winning touch was her special "Hemp Seed Dressing."

That's right, the judging has reached a new low, wherein lobster and caviar aren't a big enough bribe; now you actually have to provide these craven judges with illicit drugs. In your salad! So perhaps next year, just to cling to my pitiful third place, I'll be expected to whip up a little "Niçoise Crack Salad" with my famous "Crystal Meth Vinaigrette"!

I meditated on this sad state of affairs while walking through the van Gogh exhibit at the L.A. County Museum. There, communing with another misunderstood artist not recognized in his own time, I received inspiration. It was as though van Gogh himself had whispered in my ear. First of all he mumbled something about not "cutting off your freaking ear," which I had no intention of doing, by the way.

Then he whispered to me the perfect answer to all my salad prayers. Since I am sick to death of trying to please a certain Mrs. Peggy Keefer, I have decided that instead, next year, I will simply concoct the most hideous salad ever made and force her to eat it. Here's what I have so far: "Cathyrn's Grrl Genius Lard-Stuffed Jalapeño Salad, Nestled on

Tournedos of Domestic Dog Feces, with Grapefruit Skim Milk Dressing." I'd really like to see a certain Mrs. Peggy Keefer chow down on that! Because, alas, my salads will not survive the ages, except of course in recipe form, but the look on Mrs. Peggy Keefer's face as she eats that satanic salad will last a lifetime.

A GRRL GENIUS LITTLE PINK POST-IT

Hey, Grrl Genius!

You hate it when somebody calls you a bitch, right?

Well, don't.

There isn't a woman alive who hasn't been called a bitch at some time. The more you accomplish, the more opportunities you will have to be called a bitch. Hillary Clinton was called a bitch by Barbara Bush. Mother Teresa got ripped in *Vanity Fair* for being a pushy bitch when she wasn't cradling dying lepers in her skinny arms. I'll bet there was even some disgruntled hospital worker who referred to Karen Ann Quinlan as "that bitch in a coma," as in "I'm sick of cleaning up after that bitch in a coma in room three." If you've got a pulse, you've got bitch potential, and if not, you can always be a dead bitch.

But what you need to know about being a bitch is that it's a good thing. In old Europe, *bitch* was one of the honorific titles given to the goddess, specifically Artemis-Diana, who was the goddess of the hunt. Not coincidentally, Princess Diana was named after this same goddess and spent her short life being called a bitch by almost everyone, including the queen, who, according to the pagan English tradition where royalty are descended from the gods, could also be referred to quite properly as a genuine bitch goddess herself.

Romans worshiped the goddess Lupa, or the wolf bitch; the Great Bitch Sarama led the Vedic dogs of death. The bitch goddess was a key figure in all the Indo-European cultures for thousands of years.

And now, Grrl Genius, the bitch is back.

A GRRL GENIUS LITTLE PINK POST-IT

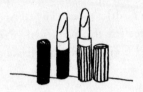

Hey, Grrl Genius!

Putting on lipstick can help you think better!

If you are stuck on a work problem, chances are that your left logical linear brain is becoming bogged down and overloaded. In order to rebalance yourself, try putting on some lipstick (I suggest Chanel Velvet Creme lipstick in Velvet Rouge, or Bobbi Brown's Mattestain in "Love 2").

The use of color, drawing skills, and artistic judgment that are required for proper lipstick application will energize your right (feminine) brain, giving your left (masculine) brain some needed time off. Switching hemispheric functions in this fashion also activates the corpus colossum, the portion of the brain that integrates the activities of both hemispheres. Even a short break of lipstick application can allow your left brain to recharge and help you to solve your work problem more effectively.

Plus, you look cuter!

A GRRL GENIUS LITTLE PINK POST-IT

Hey, Grrl Genius!

Why does the Victoria's Secret catalog make you want to kill yourself?

Because it's telling you with every glossy page that you are not good enough. The fact is that the models and actresses whom you see on TV, on magazine covers, on billboards, are generally thinner than 95 percent of the population of women. And if you're feeling worse and worse about yourself, it's not necessarily because you've changed, but because the models have changed. In the 1960s, fashion models weighed 8 percent less than the average American woman; today they weigh 23 percent less. Marilyn Monroe, the ultimate movie-star sex symbol, wore a size fourteen and would today be considered a plus-size woman.

Dieting doesn't work and only makes us fatter, thus fueling the billion-dollar dieting oligarchy. During the course of a lifetime, the average American woman loses 100 pounds on diets, and gains 125 pounds.

Barbie, perhaps the greatest American icon of female beauty, has a waist that is so thin that, if she were a real woman, she would have no internal organs whatsoever. It's fair to note that Barbie has nothing to complain about in the missing-organ department compared to Ken. But why do we want to look like Barbie? Is it for men? Do guys really walk down the street saying, "Oh, man, she looks hot, she looks like she doesn't have a liver or kidneys or islets of Langerhans or any internal organs at all! What a stone-cold fox! No spleen!"

If you don't think that these images affect you, you might like to know that Fiji Islanders recently got television for the first time. After a couple of seasons of *Baywatch*, there was a drastic rise in the number of eating disorders among teenage girls, which had been almost nonexistent in their culture before TV. Through the magic of Hollywood, people all over the world can now feel terrible about themselves.

Advertisers have created ever more impossible ideals of beauty in order to rob Grrls of their self-esteem. And why do advertisers want to rob you of your self-esteem? So they can sell it back to you, of course.

Here's an amazing fact: one sector of the female American population has completely turned their backs on the new skinny fascism—black Grrls. Although they are statistically more likely to be overweight, they like themselves better than white Grrls do. Between the ages of nine and fifteen, black female adolescents' self-esteem dropped only seven percentage points while white Grrls' dropped thirty-three points. Why do the sisters refuse to buy into the low self-esteem that Madison Avenue serves up? Maybe because Madison Avenue has spent so long pretending black Grrls don't exist that black Grrls have no trouble telling them to take their anorexia and shove it.

Black Grrl Geniuses have a head start; the rest of us need to follow in their Nubian princess footsteps. Love yourself, and tell Madison Avenue to kiss your round, luscious Grrl Genius ass!

Step Three

"Boldly Accepted Our Grrrl Genius Mortality"

I have a horror of death; the dead are so soon forgotten. But when I die, they'll have to remember me.

—EMILY DICKINSON

Just remember, we're all in this alone.

—LILY TOMLIN

I have read numerous surveys that say most people's number one fear is public speaking. Because of this, relentlessly optimistic public-speaking gurus in snappy business-wear are always encouraging reluctant public speakers to summon up their courage by "imagining your audience is in their underwear," which I know is bad advice, because I've tried it.

Maybe it doesn't work for me because I am too tender-hearted. When I look out into an audience and try to imagine them in their underwear, all I see are timid, soft-bellied men spilling out of the overstretched, gray elastic of their sad, yellowing briefs. I see the women's pendulous breasts sagging wearily against underwire as their merry, plump buttocks are cruelly squeezed, sausagelike, into control-top panty hose. The people seem ashamed, apologetic, as I openly stare at their half-nakedness. They seem to be mumbling vague promises to use the Ab Rollers and Thighmasters that clog their moldy basement rec rooms. I feel I have violated these people, turned them into objects of ridicule against their will.

These tragic lingerie images always manage to sink me into a deep depression, rendering me incapable not just of public speaking, but of doing anything more challenging than slurping cold chicken-noodle soup directly out of the can and watching *Jerry Springer* all afternoon.

Public speaking can be nerve-racking, but when it comes to number one fears, mine is always death, followed closely by being yelled at. Did the people who answered the fear survey forget about death? I am not ashamed to admit that I am plenty scared of dying. As far as death goes, I share the opinion of noted humorist Woody Allen, who once said, "It's not so much that I'm afraid of death, I just don't want to be there when it happens."

Since I realized early on that I would be there when it happens, I learned to cultivate my Grrl Genius sense of courage in the face of death by endlessly imagining the various ways I might die. The deaths I envision for myself are always chock-full of drama and not limited to the realities of space and time.

As a young high school girl back in Minnesota, I used to imagine being flayed alive by icily handsome Vikings, the coarse iron blade splitting my skin as the Viking, clad in musky animal pelts and stinking of salted fish, reaches his burly hand into my chest cavity, tossing my lungs over my shoulders to form the wings for the traditional Nordic "angel of death," as he rips out my still-beating heart and waves it before my eyes.

Sometimes I would fantasize about being executed, wrongfully of course, the electric chair being my personal favorite method. I would constantly revise the menu for my last meal, my favorite being delicately steamed Maine lobster, oysters on the half shell, and fried clams, followed by a hot fudge sundae.

I would conjure up every word of the deep, soulful last conversation I have in my dingy cell with a hunky, young priest who realizes, too late alas, that I am the one woman he would give up his vocation for, knowing that his love for God would only grow by sharing sweet connubial bliss with someone as deeply spiritual as me. As we embrace, I feel his ministerial love wand rising with desire beneath his chasuble, and unable to resist, we make torrid, sanctified love on the cold cement floor. Later, at the stroke of midnight, I feel the gigawatts of electricity burning through me as I realize that underneath my canvas hood, I am not only experiencing death, but probably the worst static flyaway hair imaginable.

Even if I imagined an everyday kind of death, it would still have plenty of pizzazz. I would picture myself blithely walking across the street, obsessing about my desperate need for a certain pair of fuchsia suede sling-backs, when I would suddenly be hit by a speeding Mack truck. I would feel the initial elation of soaring freely through the air, before becoming aware of the pain of every bone in my body being pulverized.

This constant imagining of my death seemed to reduce my constant terror of dying, or at least it made it somehow more manageable. It was my perfect Grrl Genius solution to the ultimately unsolvable problem of mortality.

Recently, I got a message on my cell phone that was mostly garbled, except for the number. I always naively assume these kind of mystery messages must be from someone randomly giving away Chanel lipsticks or beachfront real estate, and so I instantly returned the call. When I dialed the number, a loud, perky woman answered and tried to sell me preneed funeral arrangements. I had foolishly announced myself when I called, and she seized on this information, relentlessly using my name the way an unscrupulous baby-seal hunter uses a club.

"Cathryn, have you seriously considered investing in preneed funeral arrangements?"

"Well, no . . . not exactly."

"I must tell you, Cathryn, there is nothing as wonderful as the feeling of knowing that your final arrangements are completely secure."

I wondered if this woman had ever heard of chocolate or orgasms, but I decided to leave it alone. If she got that jazzed off preneed arrangements, who was I to bust up her scene?

"I'm so glad you called, Cathryn, because we have a limited number of crypt berths still available—"

"I'm just not exactly sure where I want to be buried, so I think I'll just—"

Her voice was so annoying and jarring that it had an actual physical effect on me, the sort of effect that you can usually only get by biting heartily into a giant wad of tin foil.

"Cathryn, have you ever been to a shopping center the day after Thanksgiving?"

"Well, yeah, but—"

"Have you frantically driven in circles, Cathryn, following people, hoping that they will be the ones to leave so that you can have their parking space? Of course you have. But what you have to remember is that at a cemetery, no one ever leaves their parking space; once that lot is full, that's it, Cathryn, there's no place for you to go."

I hated the idea that I suddenly had a new parking problem to contend with, and so I quickly hung up on her. Although I think about my own funeral nearly every day, my preneed arrangements are so far limited to making my hairdresser, the wizardly Bill Belshya, promise that he will give me one last color touch-up and blow-dry before anyone sees me. To be dead is a drag, to be dead with roots is intolerable. I am further annoyed by the thought that hair continues growing after death, so when I'm six feet under, I will definitely have roots. Of course, I'll also have worms and slugs crawling out of my vacant eye sockets, but that doesn't seem to worry me. For me, it's all about the hair. One of my uncles was recently forced to wait until the spring thaw to bury his mother, and when I think of that dear woman lying in a drawer with a half-grown-out perm, my heart truly bleeds.

I wondered if the preneed funeral call was a bad omen. When I got home, there was a message on my home machine saying that a good friend's husband had suddenly dropped dead. It was then that I realized that the call *was* a bad omen, just not for me.

The thing no one ever wants to admit about funerals is that each one is a near miss. No food tastes better than the food you have after a funeral, no sexual encounter is more roof-raising or star-spangled than the sex you have after a funeral. After all, the best thing about any funeral is the fact that it isn't yours.

It's not surprising that I thought a lot about death growing up in the frigid suburbs of Minnesota, a state overflowing with Swedes, the most statistically suicidal people on earth, and perhaps the only place in America where you can be cryogenically frozen just by walking from the Target to your car.

The main reason I thought a lot about death and funerals as a small child was not just my natural girlish ghoulishness, nurtured by the strange erotic pulsings I felt whenever Gomez Addams kissed his way up Morticia's slender black arm. No, the main reason was our neighbor two doors down, Jerry Green, the glamorous new stepdad of my friend Amy Dahlquist.

Jerry Green was the funeral king of Roseville, Minnesota. He was the owner of Kindler-Farber Vaults, a major player in the coffin- and vault-making game. Mr. Green, or Jerry as he groovily let us call him, was the most handsome dad in the neighborhood, a perpetually tan marathon runner with Dorian Gray–ish good looks. He was freakishly younger-looking than all the other dads; the fact that he actually *was* younger never occurred to us, we just naturally assumed it was because he drank the embalming fluid. Different of course from the embalming fluids our fathers drank, my dad's personal favorite being a Beefeater martini on the rocks with a twist, no olive.

Jerry was not only young-looking and handsome, he was odd, the sexiest thing of all. He was always declaring that he was dedicated to "putting the 'fun' back into funeral." His coffin factory was by the freeway, and over it he placed an enormous billboard that read, "Drive Carefully, We Can Wait!" He would always let Amy and her friends play hide-and-seek in the coffin warehouse, which is as scary as you imagine it would be. Every Halloween, he would set up an actual coffin in his front yard, lie in it, and make you "wake him from the dead" to get your treat. Since he always gave out full-size Snickers bars, you, of course, had no choice but to do it.

Jerry and Alice Green threw a lot of neighborhood cocktail parties in their tasteful Danish Modern house, and as an eerily festive touch, he would always use an infant casket for the ice chest. This was the move that caused my mother, a gracious-living junkie, to boycott his parties permanently. My mom will put up with a lot of crap, but don't ask her to get ice from a baby coffin or have a nice conversation over a cremation-urn centerpiece.

As if all that were not weird and exotic enough, Jerry was also a big-game hunter in Africa. The heads of various endangered species hung angrily all over their house. I remember once sitting on the toilet of Jerry and Alice's bathroom, the giant severed head of a wildebeest glaring down at me. At the time, I was reading *Funeral Monthly* and saw an ad for one of the top-of-the-line Kindler-Farber vaults. Jerry, looking bronzed and fit, was in a full-page, glossy color picture, pointing proudly to a large cement vault, one of the "Perma-Seal series." The ad copy beneath the picture asked the provocative question "Are your loved one's subject to seepage?"

As I stared at the magazine, I couldn't believe that I was sitting on the same toilet that the dashing man in the glossy color ad had sat on maybe only hours before. As far as I was concerned, anyone who had a giant color picture in a magazine was a full-on celebrity. With my twin attractions to death and fame, it's no surprise that I spent years nursing an aching, deep crush on Jerry Green. He had everything, he was exciting, he was famous, he was Gomez Addams with a tan.

Since I've never really gotten over Jerry, it should also come as no surprise that I had my first sexual experience in a graveyard. By sexual experience I don't mean the first actual intercourse, which was, of course, a big letdown.

No, the graveyard sex was that amazing "everything but" phase, the endless delicious foreplay among the headstones of Roselawn Cemetery with the straight cousin of my gay best friend, Danny Schmitz. Even though I was kissing his cousin, it was Danny who I desperately wanted to want me, but deep down I knew he never would. At the time I was caught up in the tragedy of the fact that the genuine love Danny and I had for each other would never be consummated. All these years later, it still hasn't, and I couldn't be happier about it. I am grateful that Danny, who now lives in L.A., still loves me truly and dearly, regardless of the state of my ass, which he continues to have no interest in.

I continued with my funereal fixations into adulthood. When I went to opera school in Chicago, I made a healthy part-time living singing at weddings and funerals, but funerals were always the preferred gig. No pissy brides and, especially if you could manage to squeeze out a few crocodile tears, way better tips. No one ever questioned why I was shedding tears for a stranger. Often weepy, geriatric relatives would grasp me desperately with their liver-spotted hands and make me promise to sing at their funeral too. It was an easy promise to make, because I knew that they would never know whether I had welshed on the deal and blown off the gig.

Since I was now a seasoned funeral professional, I had a cocky attitude toward the business of death. I would sit in the back rooms of funeral parlors in a chic little black dress, throwing back a few drinks, listening to the undertakers swapping stories. My favorite story was always the one of the new undertaker who was embalming a body with some air still trapped in the lungs, suddenly causing the body to sit up and say "Mama!" Every undertaker always swore that the story was true, and even though I'd heard it a gillion times, I would always pretend to believe them.

In my new role as a designated mourner, I felt tough and courageous, no longer afraid of dying because I was the girl who drinks and sings in the face of death. Of course, you can be as arrogant as you want about death, until somebody you actually know dies. When that finally happens, death starts to look like the Fonz, tough and smart in a leather jacket, and you end up looking like Ralph Malph, sloppy and stupid in a big, ugly plaid sweater.

A few years after I got out of college, my aunt Susie died. It was strange and untimely, and no one in the family has ever adequately explained, to my satisfaction, why she "just never woke up" at age forty-eight. She left behind four adorable children, three Grrl Geniuses and one Enlightened Male, and my scotch-loving Scottish uncle Bruce.

Due to the religious schizophrenia that runs through my mother's family, my aunt Susie, who was born Jewish, was due to be buried in an enormous Catholic funeral down in Virginia, which would be presided over by John Cardinal O'Connor, the virtual pope of America. I was asked to sing at the service, and I was actually glad to be able to do something useful.

Now, Susie's children, my cousins, had been raised with a deep and abiding love for the American musical theater, a cruel social handicap that I share. In their grief, this unfortunate affliction came to the surface, and they asked me to sing a couple of show tunes at the funeral. I happily agreed, confident in the fact that a full cardinal was choppering in from New York City to lower the iron fist of Catholicism on the ridiculous notion of my singing "Another Suitcase in Another Hall" from *Evita* over the deceased.

I knew I had nothing to worry about, since Catholics never allow secular music at a funeral mass. I had music charted up in my preferred key for the surefire Catholic crowd-pleasers "Ave Maria" and "Amazing Grace." I felt confident that I would, as they say, "kill" at this funeral. I would pull out all the stops, including the trademark big tear rolling out of my left eye, a little touch I had plagiarized from a picture I'd seen in an old *Life* magazine of a large black man sobbing as he played an accordion at FDR's funeral.

I got off the airplane and went to the wake, where, inspired by their mother's earthly remains, my cousins had come up with even more ridiculous song requests. They wanted the dreaded "Memory" from *Cats,* the fully hideous "Lara's Theme" from *Doctor Zhivago*, which I didn't even know had words. I even agreed to sing the excruciating "Rainbow Connection" from *The Muppet Movie.* I agreed to everything, knowing the cardinal would be as enthusiastic about my singing Muppet songs as he would be about my stripping down to pasties and a G-string and giving lap dances in the vestry.

On the morning of the funeral, I spoke to the cardinal's fey assistant about my cousins' wildly inappropriate musical requests. On hearing the list of secular songs, the wispy assistant was suitably horrified and turned as crimson as, well, a cardinal and rushed off to get the big "No way" from His Eminence. Confidently, I handed my Catholic hit-parade music to the organist.

The church was beginning to fill up with hundreds of mourners. A few minutes later, the cardinal's assistant returned, saucily flouncing his cassock like Scarlett O'Hara at a barbecue with the Tarelton twins.

He breezily informed me that "due to the extraordinary tragedy of the death, the cardinal is making an exception, and has decided to waive the usual secular-music restrictions." Apparently the Red Man had decided that puppet ballads and show tunes would be just fine after all.

It was more than I could bear, and I pushed my face in close to the cardinal's boy's and hissed, "What do you frigging mean he's 'making an exception'?"

Taken aback, the cardinal's slip of an assistant started to shake like a dashboard doll. "I'm sure there's no need for profanity," he sputtered. As if *frigging* is profanity, which everyone knows it is not.

"Well, there's no need for frigging show tunes either!"

"But the cardinal feels—" he stammered.

"Who cares what the frigging cardinal frigging feels!" Now I was overusing *frigging* because of the good effect it kept yielding, better even than if I had used real profanity, which of course I did not have the guts to do inside a Catholic church. Between what I've read about the Inquisition and all the *Godfather* movies I've seen, I knew enough about Catholicism to know that I was not about to get into it in any real way with the hierarchy of the Catholic Church. Still, I continued to plead my case. "Can't you talk to him? I mean, I can't believe he really wants me to sing all those songs, it's like some kind of horrible funeral lounge act!"

"Well, if you'd prefer not to sing, I'm sure—"

"I have no choice, these are my cousins, and I love them, and I said I'd do it for chrissake!"

Suddenly, the cardinal's boy felt emboldened. "Well, maybe you should do it, for Christ's sake."

As it always is with Catholic dogma, he had managed to trap me on a linguistic technicality, so I switched tactics.

"How can he possibly make an exception? I thought Catholics didn't make exceptions, I thought that was your whole act!"

I moved in for the kill. "But since the cardinal is feeling so warm and fuzzy and liberal, why don't you go see if he feels like making some more exceptions. How about easing up on condoms, or women priests? How about those for some exceptions?"

"The cardinal simply feels—"

I cut him off. "Oh, the cardinal can go to hell."

Well, that's what I wished I had said anyway. I never seem to pull off that kind of sass in the moment. What I actually said was something way less snarky and sarcastic, something like "I don't believe this!" accompanied by a lot of useless huffing and pouting and eye-rolling.

The funeral was long and arduous. Due to the groove-tastic 1970s architecture, I was forced to sing a dizzying succession of show tunes from the very front of the church, since there was no choir loft. Apparently offended by my comments about his boss, the cardinal's whipping boy made sure that I was constantly enveloped in a dense, acrid fog of incense that kept furiously billowing out of his censer.

The cardinal himself changed miters and stoles every five minutes, like Lola Falana at Caesars Palace. Although I was the one hacking and coughing my way through a one-woman cabaret act, I, of course, wasn't allowed so much as a freaking feather boa, or even a piano to lie on.

In the midst of all this, my uncle Bruce, well into a four-day scotch bender, decided that he wanted to do one of the Scripture readings. As he shakily made his way across the multileveled—"Hey, wouldn't this be great for a production of *Godspell*"—altar area, he tripped ever so slightly. Because of all the levels, this slight misstep mutated into a spectacular, slow-motion fall. The kind of endless, tragic fall that keeps building momentum, mostly because the person performing it refuses to accept that the fall is happening at all.

As he free-fell, my uncle Bruce started uselessly clutching anything within his reach, mostly what I can only assume were a lot of Catholic flags on big brass poles. As he continued his descent, the flags fell like dominoes, clatter-

ing loudly off the altar, the coffin, and the giant metal cru-
cifix church left.

Le cardinal and his origami-thin chorus boy managed
neatly to sidestep my uncle's spontaneous production number. Since they were apparently forbidden by their union
to have anything to do with the scenery, I was suddenly
forced to become not only head chanteuse, but stagehand
as well. Sweating profusely in my ankle-length velvet dress,
I awkwardly tried to rearrange the giant flagpoles. In the
process of cleaning up the mess, I "accidentally" knocked
over the censer, since I had two more numbers to get
through and I'd officially had enough of their papal bull.

Mercifully, the funeral mass ended and the coffin was
carried out as I sang the only appropriate number on the
bill, "Amazing Grace." I did a nice job of it, and I cried
real tears, not so much for the sorrow of the death, but just
for the general embarrassment I feel whenever I am around
people with whom I share a genetic link. Full of self-pity, I
wondered if there would ever be a time when my family
didn't humiliate me.

Before I could even finish the thought, I got my answer.
Outside the church, in a brilliant homage to Larry, Mo,
and Curly, more of my uncles, each with at least a triple
bypass to his credit, managed to drop the coffin on the lawn
of the church. Looking like a sight gag from a John Hughes
movie, the casket gaily bounced and slid on the dew-slicked
grass until it finally rested at a rakish angle near the hearse.

It was a bad funeral, and what we didn't know then was
that in less than two years my uncle would be gone too,
leaving my cousins orphaned.

Yes, it was definitely a bad funeral, but afterward I had
the most incredible Italian food, Communion-wafer–thin
slices of prosciutto on sweet casaba melon, and delicate,
garlicky pasta. After that, I flew back to L.A. and had great
sex with my husband. I realized that although it had been a

bad funeral, the best thing about it was the best thing about every funeral—it wasn't mine.

I still continue to attempt to stoke my Grrl Genius sense of courage by imagining my death, my current favorite scenario being inspired by the Los Angeles man who hitched more than a thousand helium balloons to his aluminum lawn chair and rode this impromptu "chair-iot" into the atmosphere, bringing air traffic at LAX to a standstill. Although he clearly didn't deserve to, the man survived. In my version I just ride in my lawn chair up through the stratosphere, quietly sipping on my sports bottle full of Snapple, gently passing out from lack of oxygen. I don't like to think of it as suicide; I prefer to think of it as a goofy prank gone very wrong.

I would never actually do it, of course. If I'm going to boldly accept my Grrl Genius mortality, I have to accept that I don't get to decide when the end will come. As tempting as it is to strap Mylar balloons to one's lounge chair, I know that it's not right. It's not fair to all the people I love, who have avoided the temptations of helium themselves.

Fantasizing about funerals is still a pastime, but it has gotten less amusing as the reality of planning funerals has gotten more imminent. A few years ago, my dad had a quintuple bypass. When they wheeled him out of surgery, his normally tan face looked ashen and waxy, and I almost passed out from the realization that in all likelihood I would be in charge of burying him one day.

Since my mother is so quiet and dependable, I never worry about having to bury her. I feel quite certain that she will somehow bury me off, the same way she married me off, in perfect style and with a lot of poise.

My father is so goofy that I just can't imagine him ever dying. I remember walking down Michigan Avenue with him when I was at college in Chicago, back in the go-go eighties. Every few minutes he would loudly and inexplicably say the word "Beep!" He told me that he had resolved to say "Beep!" every time he saw a businessman wearing the latest fad, a garish yellow tie. After a lifetime of wearing tasteful rep ties chosen by my tasteful mother, he couldn't believe that anyone would wrap "a goddamn piss-yellow piece of cloth" around his neck.

My dad hated the yellow ties and calmly explained that due to their extreme ugliness, he believed the ties were a symbol of an international conspiracy, some sort of dastardly secret fraternal order, and he wanted the offending tie wearers to know that he was onto their game. It all seemed perfectly logical to him, and he continued beeping like that for years, until the piss-yellow ties thankfully fell out of fashion.

Despite the fact that for my whole life my father's been in and out of the hospital with diabetes, heart disease, tumors, I cling to the notion that his sheer wackiness guarantees that he will live forever. I know it's not true, but it's a convenient lie I tell myself.

Sometimes I feel so much love for my parents, people I prefer to make fun of, that it makes my breath come ragged and raspy in my throat. To watch my dad gently lift his six-year-old grandson into his fishing boat on a sparkling summer day is an annoyingly real reminder that some people are old, and some people are young, and everybody is going to check out.

My dad recently got a present from one of my orphaned cousins. It's a hideous, tacky plastic plaque that has what appears to be a stuffed largemouth bass mounted on it. When you push a button, the plaque begins playing the song "Take Me to the River" as the plastic bass starts flipping its tail against the plaque in perfect time to the music. As the music gets more intense, the fish's head deftly swivels toward the viewer, and its lips start moving, as the large mouth of the bass effortlessly lip-synchs to the lyric "Take me to the river . . . drop me in the water!"

My father loves this fish plaque beyond all reason. Randomly, he'll walk over to the mantelpiece, where the plaque sits next to my mother's elegant, handmade Ukrainian ostrich egg, and he'll push the fish's button, gleefully watching as it sings, "Take me to the river . . . drop me in the water!"

My dad watches the fish with the childish expression of sheer joy that you always see on one of those Make a Wish kids who has just been granted his dying dream of going to Disneyland. Watching my dad watching his fish, I feel angry and frightened that I can love anyone that fiercely.

There are a lot of things I don't know about death, mine or others', but I do know that my dad's singing fish is going to be the star attraction at his funeral. As a Grrl Genius who accepts my mortality, and the mortality of the people I love, I want my dad's funeral to perfectly reflect his brilliant goofiness, and believe me, nothing would say it better than having that weird crazy singing fish belting out a tune. If our prissy Episcopalian priest thinks that's too tacky, too "secular," I will simply tell him that he can go to hell. And this time I really will say it.

DIAGRAM OF A GRRL GENIUS BRAIN
BEFORE AND AFTER
THE TWELVE STEPS OF THE GRRL GENIUS PROGRAM

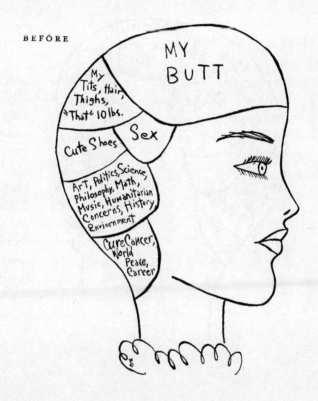

BEFORE

AFTER

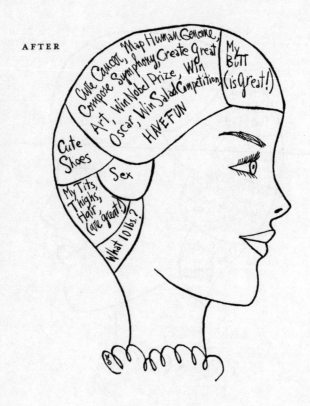

A GRRL GENIUS LITTLE PINK POST-IT

Hey, Grrl Genius!

Remember when they told you in school that Eli Whitney invented the cotton gin? They were stinking liars! Oh, sure, Eli Whitney has the patent on the cotton gin, but the woman who owned the boardinghouse he lived in actually invented the stupid thing.

Catherine Littlefield Greene, who had five kids and a dead husband, was sick to death of picking seeds out of the cotton she had to spin to make clothes. So Catherine, in between cooking grits and changing diapers, drew up detailed plans for a machine and asked her boarder Eli to build it, on account of he was kind of handy and she was way too busy. At first, Eli tried to make the machine with wooden teeth, which didn't work at all, so she told him to use wire, and of course it worked like a charm.

Eli Whitney then stole her plans, got the patent on the cotton gin, and single-handedly started up the slave economy of the Old South.

Catherine Littlefield Greene continued whomping up biscuits at her boardinghouse and being a single mom to her five children.

The lesson is, don't give away your genius!

A GRRL GENIUS FACTETTE

Spa treatments can help you live longer!

According to the authors of the book *Real Age,* the use of hot tubs, saunas, steam rooms, etc., has a beneficial and detoxifying effect that could make your physical age up to 4.5 years younger than your chronological age.

Furthermore, owning a Jacuzzi spa tub is not a frivolous expense; it could literally save your life in a natural diaster.

On May 3, 2000, Kelly Stover of Tulsa, Oklahoma, saw on the television that a twister was headed to her part of town. She quickly herded her husband and two small children into their luxurious spa bathtub, where they huddled with pillows and blankets. The twister ripped the roof off their house and deposited the entire family, snug in their spa tub, in the middle of their backyard, totally unscathed. Their house was completely decimated, but that spa tub saved their lives.

I'd like to see a big-screen TV top that.

"We Committed Ourselves to Our Grrl Genius Relationship (or Didn't)"

Sometimes I wonder if men and women really suit each other. Perhaps they should live next door and just visit now and then.

—KATHARINE HEPBURN

Never go to bed mad; stay up and fight.

—PHYLLIS DILLER

The world is my husband.

—ELSA MAXWELL

Admittedly, this is the weak step in my twelve-step program. I won't lie about it and will admit that right from the start. As a Grrl Genius, I want to believe in the possibility of lifelong happiness in a monogamous relationship, but I don't see a lot of good examples of that. So I turn my gaze to the natural world. I look to the graceful swan, with her Audrey Hepburn–like neck. I don't look to Audrey Hepburn herself, who endured a string of abusive marriages.

The swan mates for life, we are told. Unfortunately, swans are the meanest birds alive. A swan kicked my ass when I was in a canoe once; apparently I got too near its nest, but who's to say that all that anger was really directed at me? Who's to say that that swan hadn't just had yet another ridiculous fight with her mate? Maybe it was the fifteenth time her husband had sent her out for straw for the nest while he sat on his downy butt doing the swan equivalent of a crossword puzzle. Maybe as a result she felt the need to open up a can of "swan whup ass" on me just to vent.

To say that marriage counseling is painful is an understatement, it's like saying that performing surgery without anesthesia is painful. When I go for marriage counseling, I go with my husband to a faux-Southwestern office, a style of home furnishing I find aggressively offensive. I would like to meet the decorator who decided that the ultimate comforting knickknack for depressives would be the skull of a cow whose sorry bones were blanched white by the blistering sun, after scavengers had picked its starved carcass clean. I would like to wrap the decorator snugly in a peach-and-turquoise comforter and drop the decorator off Santa Monica Pier. The skull and the hideously insincere pastels of crying Hopi Indian chiefs are only the beginning of the assaults on my dignity that will occur in this office.

After the initial decor attack, the brain repairman usually stares at us for a few seconds, in that totally up-front way that small children like to stare at you. Then he whips out a scalpel, opens our chest cavities, and lays our internal organs out on the knotty-pine coffee table, where they are picked over and discussed and palpated for fifty minutes until they are raw and oozing. Then they are shoved back into our respective chest cavities. We are then expected to drive ourselves away and get on with our day. That's what it feels like to me.

Perhaps I am being paranoid. That's a distinct possibility, according to the Minnesota Multiphasic Personality Inventory, which was administered to me by the brain repairman. According to the results of my testing, I tend to be paranoid. And I'm willing to move past that, if everyone else is willing to stop picking on me.

I have serious doubts about this test. It is five hundred and something true-or-false questions, and it seems pretty easy to figure out what they're going for. For example, the test asks, "True or false: I enjoy puttering in my garden and picking flowers."

True.

"True or false: The voice of Satan speaks to me through my car radio and instructs me to kill, kill, kill!"

Obviously, true. What is the point?

While I have been going through this difficult time, I have been lucky enough to get a very pleasant job writing for a network television show called *Diagnosis Murder*, starring Dick Van Dyke. I have had a crush on him both as Rob Petrie and as the dancing guy in *Mary Poppins*.

Since I've had the murder job, the routine goes something like this. My husband and I begin our day with one of our usual arguments, then I head over to the offices of *Diagnosis Murder*, where I spend my day planning out a murder. It turns out I am pretty good at it. The people at the TV show have been surprised at the many clever ways I have thought of to kill another human being. What the people at the TV show don't know is that this is basically free money to me. At this point in my sad life, I would just be home planning a murder, so I might as well go to an office and plan a murder and get paid for it.

Anybody who has been married who says they have never thought of murder is a liar. Even if your marriage is going well, there are times when you just kind of wish the other person would die. Buying life insurance is the normal, accepted way of getting these feelings out.

Life insurance traces its history back to the tontine, a clever seventeenth-century invention of an Italian banker named Lorenzo Tonti. The tontine is a sort of sick lottery, in which a group of people pool their money and the last one alive gets all the loot. The experts will tell you that life insurance is sound financial planning, but I say it's just a small, demented lottery for you and your spouse. Personally, I'm all in favor of it. I'm always in favor of the lesser vice. For example, watching *Jerry Springer* is bad, but it's better than being a guest on *Jerry Springer*.

Since I have been emotionally upset recently, I have developed some bad habits. I recently became addicted to Krispy Kreme doughnuts, which was a shock, because I had never had a doughnut dependency of any kind. However, Krispy Kreme is different, or rather, Krispy Krack as I like to refer to it.

Our brain repairman suggested that my husband and I needed to share our interests with each other more. So one night, after we had gone to a show, I pleaded with my husband to drive us out to the dark wilderness of the San Fernando Valley, where the only Los Angeles Krispy Kreme factory/store is.

It was almost midnight, and we got lost. For the first time in our marriage, my husband decided he would ask for directions. Before I looked up to try to stop him, there he was, asking two LAPD cops where we could find the doughnut place. Let me make this clear, LAPD cops. The LAPD cops of Rodney King fame. The same cops who are now being civilly sued for billions of dollars for beating people senseless just for looking at them sideways. Yes, my husband, God bless him, was asking the world's touchiest cops where to find doughnuts. If we had been black, we would now be dead, of that I am sure.

But since we weren't black, the cops just grudgingly gave us directions to the Krispy Kreme.

We got to the Krispy Kreme and saw the throngs of jittery addicts waiting for their fix. People in their bathrobes driving minivans were lined up around the block at the drive-through; in the backseats were bleary-eyed children in footy pajamas who had been lifted from their beds and hastily shoved into car seats.

What is the cause of this mania? When you first bite into a Krispy Kreme doughnut, the answer is obvious. You are biting into a brilliant concoction of solid sugar and fat. These doughnuts are saturated with enough fat to make your heart stop cold, and enough sugar to make your fillings sing. At the factory, each Krispy Kreme doughnut floats gently along a beautiful golden river of hot fat, then passes slowly through a cascading waterfall of sugar. It is then coated with a sugar glaze and potentially injected with more sugar in the form of filling.

These doughnuts are the very anesthesia I am not allowed at my weekly vivisection at the brain repairman's office. It is, as Dick Van Dyke's friend Mary Poppins would say, the proverbial spoonful of sugar that makes the medicine go down.

How did I, an actual Grrl Genius, get to a place where I am wandering around my home at 1 A.M., whacked on fat and sugar, contemplating murder, and not just for my job?

I met my husband right after I got out of college. He was a stage manager and I was a chorus girl in an Off-

Broadway musical production of *Once Upon a Mattress* that toured India and Sri Lanka, Jordan and Egypt. There was a civil war in Sri Lanka, complete with machine-gun fire in the hills. As the tour went on, there was an international terrorist incident and the tour broke up. It was like something out of one of those old MGM musicals of the forties, which I have always loved. When people ask me good places to meet a husband, I say, "Singing show tunes in India." It's all I know.

And now it's a decade later, and it feels like we are mortal enemies. I do not understand how this happened. That is a job for the brain repairman.

Not long after our fateful trip to the Krispy Kreme factory, my husband and I separated.

The man who is now my estranged husband claims that I am using these doughnuts as a substitute for sex, which is a very simplistic way to look at it. Being a Grrl Genius, I must look at this question more deeply, even if I accept this leaden, linear logic that says if a woman is driving out to the heart of the San Fernando Valley at midnight looking for something hot and sweet and cream-filled, it must be some sort of sexual substitute. Even if the doughnuts *are* a substitute for sex, I ask the deeper, more probing question, what is the sex a substitute for?

Sex itself is a substitute for God. When we desire another human being sexually, we are really only trying to fill our longing for ecstasy and union with the infinite. This is why at the ultimate moment we cry out, "Oh, God!" Using the transitive principle, I conclude that the doughnuts are in fact a substitute for the divine. The doughnuts fill the endless gaping maw that is my soul's aching for unity, for meaning, for the rapture of God's all-encompassing love.

Oh, fine, maybe they're a substitute for sex. So what.

Not long after we separated, I went to New York City to

perform in a backers' audition of a new musical that is bound for the Broadway stage. The musical was written in part by my best friend from second grade, Danny Schmitz, with whom I starred in the sixth-grade production of *The Wizard of Oz*, thereby prefiguring his lifetime of gayness and my lifetime love of gay men.

I was thrilled to be in New York, thrilled to be doing a musical, and thrilled that the wonderful island of Manhattan has Krispy Kremes aplenty.

The musical we were rehearsing is based on the story of the man who rescued baby Jessica McClure from the bottom of a well in Midland, Texas, and is entitled *Oh Well*. As with all musicals, the premise of this particular show is either the greatest or the stupidest idea ever devised. Before you say that it's a stupid idea, please remember a little musical with the deeply lame title *Cats*, not even *Cats!* *Cats* is a musical about a bunch of raggedy-assed felines that can't do any of the tricks performed daily by even the laziest of house cats, cats that can't even lick their own genitals. *Cats* is a musical that made more money than the gross national product of several Scandinavian countries. For information on how to invest in the Broadway production of *Oh Well*, please see the "Grrl Genius Appendix" at the end of this book.

One night, after rehearsal for *Oh Well*, I was performing at the Comic Strip. A bunch of my friends from the *Oh Well* cast came to see me. By way of perking me up, they told me that there was a Krispy Kreme just around the corner from the club, on Seventy-eighth Street and Third Avenue. Because New York is the greatest city on earth, I was sure that the Krispy Kreme would be open twenty-four hours, and so I confidently went with my friends to a bar, where they foolishly planned to use alcohol to lift them from their earthly cares. I waited patiently, knowing that the relief from my pain would actually be found in the Kreme.

We got to the doughnut shop at twelve-fifteen and found out that it was closed. I was devastated, pounding on the glass, waving twenty-dollar bills, trying desperately to get the minimum-wage keepers of the Kreme to take pity on me. Finally one of them came out onto the sidewalk. Here is the transcript of our dialogue:

Kreme Man: We're freakin' closed, okay?

Me: I know, but why? I mean, this is New York City, the city that never sleeps, right? How can you be closed?

Kreme: Look, if you want, you could always go to the one down on Eighth Street, they're open till two. (He gives me a receipt, which has the address.)

Me: Oh, that's so great! Thank you so much! Really, thanks!

Kreme: Yeah, sure, whatever. (The door of the Krispy Kreme slams shut.)

My friends had all watched my doughnut panic attack with concern, but were kind enough not to make a big deal out of it. As my terror subsided, I started to wonder if maybe I had become just a little too dependent on these doughnuts and vowed that it was definitely something I would take a look at, at some later date.

I was at Seventy-eighth Street on the East Side, and I had to go down to Eighth Street in the East Village, then back up to 106th Street on the West Side where I was staying with my friends Mark and Ileen. What this meant was that I basically had to circumnavigate the island of Manhattan for a doughnut, but that did not seem wrong to me. In fact, it seemed symbolic, circling the island in search of the doughnut, a circle within a circle, the circle of life, something like that.

Oddly enough, none of my friends wanted to go with me; they mumbled something about my behavior being "scary." I promised that I would get lots of doughnuts and bring them to rehearsal.

"Doughnuts for everyone!" I proclaimed as I got into my cab, my golden chariot that would bring me to the golden river of fat, where redemption always waits in the form of fried dough. I snuggled into the seat, secure in the knowledge that I was in the greatest city on earth, where I would soon get the greatest doughnut on earth. Life seemed, well, sweet.

I got to Eighth Street, and I asked the driver to wait. As I crossed the dark street, heading for the temple of the Kreme, I saw that it was closed. Closed!

It's not possible! I thought. There are people inside! The guy on Seventy-eighth Street said they were open!

I pounded on the window, but the doughnut acolytes in their little paper hats pretended to neither see nor hear me. I became more agitated. I began to yell out, "The guys on Third Avenue said you were open till two! You're supposed to be open till two!"

Finally, one of people of the Kreme, a doughnut-shaped man with flame-red hair, came to the tearstained window, where I was pounding away.

"Listen, sister, it's Thursday, we're only open till two on the weekends!"

I protested, "But the guy on Third Avenue said—"

"The guy on Third Avenue is full of shit, lady."

Just then I felt a tap on my shoulder. I whirled around to see a homeless man. He was draped in yards of pleated fabric, except that on closer inspection it became apparent that what was forming the folds in the fabric was not pleats, but moistened dirt that had dried, creating the sort of fabulous textural effect you only see on the runways of Paris or in the alleyways of the East Village. His face was also cracked with dirt, and two little dribbles of frozen mucus running out of his nose looked oddly like melted candle wax. He looked like nothing so much as one of those giant troll candles people sell at Grateful Dead concerts.

The giant trolly candle man leaned in close and grabbed my arm, "Hey," he growled at me, "it happens. People lie."

I was instantly struck by the truth of what he was saying. I thought of all the lies that had landed me in front of this very Krispy Kreme. The lying man at the other Krispy Kreme, the lie of a happy marriage that was no longer happy.

I was lost in this reverie when trolly candle man recaptured my attention first with the insistent tug of his hand, and then with the hot, foul breeze of his breath. His breath was formed of the kind of putrid, rancid fumes that can only come from a lifetime of tooth decay. I then realized that he was reaching his hand out to me, and in his hand was clutched a single, crumpled dollar bill.

Yes, that's right, a homeless man was trying to give me money.

"Here," he says. "Go ahead, take it, you're havin' a rough night."

In truth, I didn't realize just what a rough night I was having until the filthy, snot-encrusted trolly candle man thought that his night was actually pretty good compared to mine. Of course, I couldn't take money from a homeless person, but he would not relent. In his view of things, I was more pathetic than he. And who was I to say he was wrong?

After all, he wasn't the one sobbing and pounding on windows begging for doughnuts. I finally took the crumpled dollar and skulked back to my cab. As I stepped in, the trolly candle man shouted out, "Don't let the goddamned bastards get you down," as he headed back to his Dumpster, or wherever he called home.

It was then I realized that I loved my trolly candle man. I loved him for trying to take care of me. I thought to myself, He is my knight in urine-soaked armor. I started wondering about his life, about our life together. I tried to visualize his Dumpster pied-à-terre, which is in a gorgeous neighborhood by the way, and started to think that it might, in fact, be nicer than many of the apartments I've seen here. At least his Dumpster is in Manhattan; it's not like he lives in a Dumpster in Queens.

Once I got back in the cab, I was fuming. One of the great things about taxicabs is that they give you license to mutter. You can mutter and rave to yourself in a taxicab just the same as if you were in a padded cell at Bellevue, and nobody thinks anything of it. Both you and the cabbie know that you are raving like the madwoman of Chaillot, but you both pretend that you are having a "conversation."

"I can't believe he told me the Krispy Kreme was open on Eighth Street, when he knows good and well they're not!" I muttered.

"Is it fun?" my rant continued. "Is it fun to delude someone into blowing an extra ten bucks on a cab downtown? Is it exciting to delude an innocent person who just happens to need a few doughnuts?"

All cabdrivers in New York have cell phones now, and they all talk on them constantly in their festive native tongues. At this point my cabbie began talking on his cell phone, thus ending our "conversation." My cabbie's name was Abdalla Shabazz, and I noticed that his native tongue involved an almost constant gagging, and scraping of the back of his throat. Conversations in his language sound exactly like a pack of feral cats collectively trying to choke up their fur balls. Every time he spoke, all I could think of was cats. I began to wonder if perhaps it was during a cab ride like this that Andrew Lloyd Webber was actually inspired to write his billion-dollar spectacle *Cats*.

Even though I didn't speak Abdalla's hair-ball-coughing language, I managed to make out some of the conversation due to his use of English words as well. It went something like this:

"AchhhACK LAchhhhGAK, Krispy Kreme, gachh-hachhgachh, doughnut, aaaakhkhkhkhkhhhhh . . . Krispy Kreme doughnut."

Abdalla is trying to save me! I thought. He is asking his other cabbies where he can find me the Krispy Kremes I so desperately need, I am sure of it.

Slowly, I became less sure of it. The thought occurred to me that, yes, Abdalla might be trying to help me, or he might just be making fun of me with his friends.

When the cab made no detours and dropped me at 106th Street, I knew for sure that Abdalla was just making fun of me. I know it's silly, but my feelings were hurt, and besides, I was still jonesing very hard for those goddamn doughnuts.

I went into the apartment, where I slept fitfully, dreaming that I was swimming in the golden river of fat at the Krispy Kreme factory. I began to be pulled under, and so I tried desperately to grab a hold of the doughnuts, thinking that I would use them as deep-fried life preservers. I couldn't get a grip and kept sliding off the doughnuts, eventually drowning in that beautiful golden river of fat.

Despite my dark and desperate dreams I woke up the next day filled with hope. After all, another day, another doughnut. Besides, a thought had occurred to me: possibly Abdalla wasn't making fun of me, but was trying to help me and was just unsuccessful.

I became thrilled with this idea and called enough of the Kremes to discover that none were open past midnight. Abdalla was trying to help me find an open Kreme, it's just that he was unsuccessful!

Filled with renewed hope about Abdalla and the basic goodness of humankind, I decided to walk to Columbus

Avenue and Seventy-second Street, where there is a Krispy Kreme. I figured I'd get three dozen doughnuts and take them to rehearsal. Normally I reserve eating the doughnuts for the hours of lowest self-esteem, between midnight and 3 A.M. Since my dark night of the Kreme had ended, I felt the need to celebrate.

I got to the Krispy Kreme on Seventy-second with plenty of time to catch a cab for rehearsal. I walked in the door, and a workman greeted me. He told me that as of twenty minutes ago this particular store had been closed for renovations.

Joan of Arc had a vision and then heard the voice of Saint Catherine in her garden. Saint Catherine told Joan to rescue the Dauphin and help him ascend to the throne of France. I always wanted to have visions, but God never seems to want to send them to me. It wasn't until my marriage started to fall apart that I finally started having visions.

The first vision happened in Santa Barbara. I was spending the weekend with my friend Pam, and I was obsessing about my failing marriage, as usual. Pam was telling me that I have to do what's right for me and accept it and move on.

"Look," Pam said, taking a healthy bite out of one of the chocolate-glazed, Bavarian Kreme Krispy Kreme doughnuts I had brought with me from L.A., "if you do get divorced, and you become bitter about it, your life is going to be ruined."

I was only half listening, concentrating as I was on reaching my index finger deep into the secret cavern of my own Bavarian Kreme doughnut.

"Don't be bitter," I repeated dully, having just hit the mother load of Kreme. I scooped out a big glob of the cocaine-white frosting and eagerly sucked it off my finger. There was nothing like mainlining Kreme. I felt the electric buzz of the sucrose right away.

"I'm serious about this bitterness thing," Pam continued. "You have to admit you have a problem with that. I
mean, look at how worked up you get about the live-salad-
making competition."

"Oh, please, like that's my fault. I mean, if it weren't
for that ignorant hack judge Mrs. Peggy Keefer—"

"But you're not bitter of course."

I stopped myself; maybe she had a point.

"Look," Pam said. "You just have to trick yourself into
being happy no matter what. If you really are a Grrl
Genius, you should be able to do it."

Suddenly, into my mind popped the image of a dog I'd
known back in our summer vacations on Cape Cod: a
golden retriever who lived up the block who had gotten
cancer in his hind leg. The owners of the dog were told that
they could put the dog down, or they could amputate the
leg. They decided to let the dog live, and for years and years
I saw that three-legged dog running on the beach, blissfully
unaware that anything was different. It was apparent that
the dog didn't even remember having had four legs and
didn't mind its three-legged state in the slightest.

I realized that, whatever happened with my marriage, I
would have to be like that three-legged dog. I would have to
forget what had come before and just function exactly as
though things were always this three-legged way. Because a
marriage is a part of you, a part of your life, and if it ends,
well, it is an amputation, of a sort.

"I just have to imagine I'm like the three-legged dog!"
I exclaimed.

Pam was used to my non sequiturs. "Whatever it takes.
If pretending you're a crippled dog does it for you, then by
all means, go for it."

The next day, I had my first vision. I took a walk on the
beach near her house and I saw it, a three-legged dog, running along the beach, just as if I had conjured it up.

The thing is, I know all the dogs on that beach, and suddenly there it was, a happy three-legged dog where there had been no three-legged dog before. Surely, I thought, this vision was a message from God that no matter what happened, I could be happy, if I wanted to.

I thought about that three-legged dog as I sat despondently outside the Krispy Kreme on Seventy-second Street that was so cruelly closed for renovations. I understood what the message of the dog was, but what was the message in this endless futile quest for the doughnuts? Was the message that God wanted me to be more grateful for the abundance in my life? Was the message that the only way to get what I wanted was to stop wanting it so desperately? Was the message that I should stop eating so many doughnuts? After all, sometimes a burning bush is a sign from God, and sometimes it's just a sign that you need to trim your hedge more often.

Later that day I was walking with my friend Michael, coming out of the *Oh Well* rehearsal. I was talking with him about the three-legged dog, and how it was a sign that I could find happiness no matter what happened. My happiness depended on my attitude.

"If I really am a Grrl Genius, I have to realize that it's not about what I've lost, it's about what I have," I told him, sounding like one of those perky life experts I love to watch on *Oprah*.

Michael nodded and smiled in that sympathetic way people do when their miserable friends are talking about how happy they are eventually going to be.

I kept rambling on, quoting from every decoupaged plaque I'd ever seen. "The thing is, you've got to have an attitude of gratitude. When life hands you lemons, you've just got to whip up some lemonade."

I was about to launch into the old saw about "keeping your eye upon the doughnut, and not upon the hole," when I saw it, my second vision.

I looked up, and there, right before me, was a glowing, pulsing light. It was . . . the "Hot!" sign of a Krispy Kreme doughnut factory. Right in front of me, on a street I had walked down twice already. Doughnuts! My Krispy Kreme doughnuts that had been there, all along.

The message in the whole doughnut escapade was finally clear. I learned, just as I had learned in that sixth-grade production of *The Wizard of Oz*, that if I ever go searching for my heart's desire, I should look no farther than my own backyard, or in this case, just around the corner from the rehearsal hall. Happiness, in all its forms, but particularly in the form of hot, glazed doughnuts, comes to you only when you stop searching for it.

As a Grrl Genius, it's important to use your genius to decide yourself whether a relationship is right for you. Commit to your Grrl Genius relationship, or don't. But the one Grrl Genius relationship you absolutely must commit to is your relationship with yourself. That's the one you can count on.

The things that happened to me on my doughnut quest, my dark night of the dough, brought me a little closer to understanding the vague mysteries of my own heart. As for the answers to the big questions—such as, what is love? Why does it always hurt so much?—despite my genius I remain completely clueless. However, the most important thing that I learned was this:

Krispy Kremes are really, really good doughnuts.

Sister Wendy

A GRRL GENIUS PROFILE IN EXCELLENCE

(Also a shameless way of sucking up to a celebrity
I would give anything to meet)

Sister Wendy, host of her own eponymous, highly rated
art-appreciation show on PBS, is the hottest nun to blaze
onto the pop cultural scene since Sister Bertrille.

A cloistered nun in England, Sister Wendy regularly
appears on American television in full nun drag to gleefully
guide viewers with her Grrl Genius through the world of
fine art. She lingers particularly on the sensual aspects of
painting, blithely discussing Leonardo da Vinci's homosexuality one minute and the next minute exclaiming about
the "lovely and fluffy pubic hairs" on a Stanley Spencer like
no nun you ever heard.

Sister Wendy began her study of art by having friends
send her art postcards to her isolated trailer home outside
a Carmelite convent. She then studied art history at
Oxford and began publishing scholarly papers on art that
had a wonderfully human touch.

She was subsequently given her own show on PBS, a full hour of art discussion with no script or preparation. Sister Wendy, like Sister Bertrille, wings it.

Sister Wendy is not only a brilliant art scholar, she is an extremely fun nun who could single-handedly resurrect the whole notion of nuns for recovering Catholics everywhere. When asked by Bill Moyers about guilt, Sister Wendy replied, "Guilt is a ridiculous emotion, completely useless; contrition, now that is something that makes sense." A nun who thinks guilt is a waste of time, how geniusy is that?

When asked about Serrano's sculpture *Piss Christ,* a work that features crucufixes floating dreamily in a jar of human urine, Sister Wendy didn't bat an eye and replied, "It isn't great art, but it's very good art. I think what the artist is saying is that nothing can dilute the message of Jesus." Not even piss! Sister Wendy rocks!

Sister Wendy, with her wonderful exuberance and fantastic overbite, is using her vast Grrl Genius to bring a new understanding of the world's greatest art treasures to couch potatoes across the globe.

Sister Wendy, I love you, and your Grrl Genius!

A GRRL GENIUS LITTLE PINK POST-IT

Hey, Grrl Genius!

Did you know that you *need* chocolate? You *need* it! And there is a giant conspiracy trying to prevent you from having it!

In her now out-of-print work of sheer, mind-bending brilliance, *Why Women Need Chocolate,* noted nutritionist and Grrl Genius Deborah Waterhouse outlines why chocolate is an absolutely necessary part of good female nutrition. According to Miss Waterhouse, 97 percent of all women report food cravings and the number one food they crave is chocolate. Is it because 97 percent of women are weak-willed, slovenly idiots, or because they are Grrl Geniuses who crave what they absolutely need to survive?

Here are some chocolate-covered facts:

* Chocolate has a blend of over five hundred flavors, two and a half times more than *any other food.*

* Grrls are twenty-two times more likely than men to choose chocolate as a mood enhancer.

* Chocolate contains phenylethylamine, the chemical that is released in the brain when we fall in love.

* Chocolate contains theobromine, which increases alertness, concentration, and cognitive functioning.

* Chocolate contains magnesium, essential to manufacturing serotonin.

* Due to its ideal ratio of fat-to-sugar calories, chocolate boosts serotonin and endorphin levels in the brain.

* These brilliant and unique chemical components of chocolate make its use the ideal solution to hormonal mood swings. Chocolate is potentially more powerful, and certainly more tasty, than such serotonin reuptake inhibitors as Prozac and Zoloft, which are expensive and diminish sexual response.

* Fifty percent of all women say they would choose chocolate over sex.

But you don't have to choose! As a Grrl Genius you can have both chocolate and sex!

Your cravings for chocolate are not a sign of weakness, they are a sign of your body's innate, subconscious Grrl Genius. Just as with women in Thailand who eat rotting wood when they are pregnant in order to ingest the wood fungus that provides them with essential B vitamins, your craving for chocolate is a sign of your body's inherent wisdom.

Eat chocolate, and take a B-vitamin pill, as rotting-wood fungus is not that easy to find, and not that tasty once you find it.

Unless you cover it in chocolate!

Important questions that must be asked include:

Why didn't Deborah Waterhouse win the Nobel Prize?

Who gives a lab rat's ass about mapping the human genome compared to the life-altering information that "women *need* chocolate"?

Why did Deborah Waterhouse's stunning work of paradigm-smashing genius go out of print?

Is it possible that an evil cabal of pharmaceutical companies that stand to make billions of dollars on prescription antidepressants could collude and conspire to make one little book suddenly go "out of print"?

Did you know that women are twice as likely to be prescribed antidepressants as men?

Would it be worth it to make one book go out of print so that millions of women will feel guilty about eating chocolate so that billions of dollars could be made by turning women who just need some freaking M&M's into prescription-drug junkies?

You're the Grrl Genius, you be the judge.

Just say yes to chocolate!

"Came to Believe That a Grrl Genius Works Well with Others"

Our struggle is not to have a female Einstein get appointed
to assistant professor. It is for a woman schlemiel
to get as quickly promoted as a male schlemiel.

—BELLA ABZUG

Success didn't spoil me, I've always
been insufferable.

—FRAN LEBOWITZ

Obviously, the ideal work situation for any budding Grrl Genius is to be an heiress, freed from the cruel constraints of petty commerce. In this rarefied environment, her genius can be tended and nurtured like a delicate, pink hothouse orchid. Unfortunately, heiress gigs are notoriously hard to line up, notwithstanding the whole New Age notion that as free-floating soul blobs, we "choose" our parents when we decide to incarnate into earthly form. I mean, God bless my folks, but I'm no dummy. If I'd had a choice I'd have picked me some du Ponts, or maybe a nice Coppola, thus getting both fame and money connections all at once.

I narrowly missed my chance to be an heiress when my father's father, a brilliant inventor, signed a contract with Western Union stipulating that he hand over his patents in exchange for a nice middle-class salary during the dark years of the Depression. Among his inventions was a design for a photocopy machine, which Western Union deemed to be not even worth patenting, given the existence of the highly dependable mimeograph machine.

Obviously, the executives at Western Union were high on the Depression-era equivalent of crack. This was a colossal corporate error along the lines of if Henry Ford had decided not to get into the car business on account of the dependability of the horse and buggy. If things had gone differently, if my grandfather had been out on his own, you'd be standing in line at Kinko's waiting to "Michon" your tax forms, and I'd be riding around in a golden, diamond-encrusted sedan chair. At the very least, if Western Union had fully grasped my grandfather's brilliance, Western Union would be a worldwide conglomerate with gleaming office towers, instead of the best way to send money to bail your drug-addict friends out of the pokey.

If you can't be a Grrl Genius heiress, you'll obviously

have to work. The pain of this horrible reality can be deadened considerably if you use some of my easy but effective Grrl Genius Career Coping Tools.

Grrl Genius Career Coping Tool #1:

Recreational Job Bashing

This tool, almost more than any other, will launch you on the path to Grrl Genius career success. Recreational job bashing, or RJB, is an important job-survival skill for all Grrl Geniuses to learn. In essence, recreational job bashing means that in addition to your chosen field, you become a part-time critic of the way that everyone else is doing his or her job. Relishing the ineptitude of someone else's job performance is key to helping you survive and thrive in your own job.

For example, in a recent recreational-job-bashing session, I enjoyed myself immensely by reading the many hundreds of glossy pages devoted to the pregnancy, birth, and postpartum recovery of supermodel Cindy Crawford. Giving birth is an honorable profession, but magazine editors were acting as though Cindy Crawford had invented the whole concept of being a mammal. The coverage of this blessed event couldn't have been more exhaustive if it had taken place in a Bethlehem manger and been attended by myrrh-bearing wise guys. It has spawned a whole "Cindy Tested, Cindy Approved" birthing industry. After all, who better to be a spokesperson for beleaguered new moms than a billionaire supermodel?

If you are wondering how to get through the day on three hours of sleep, just ask Cindy how she manages with only a SWAT-team-sized household staff. Cindy has also been more than happy to share her experience, strength, and hope about losing that pesky pregnancy weight. Apparently, as a genetic super Lotto winner, it has been no trouble at all! Just eat right, exercise, and be a supermodel. Why on earth didn't you think of that, gentle magazine reader, huddled in your double-wide house trailer, desperately trying to wedge yourself into your prepregnancy jeans as your baby screams himself hoarse? Where are your nannies and personal trainers and yoga gurus? Did you foolishly forget to pick them up at the Wal-Mart, instead recklessly wasting your money on diapers and canned goods?

If I ran the women's magazines (this is a key element of recreational job bashing, you must always be the person in charge), my TV agent Terry would be the cover mom of the hour. Gorgeous in a normal way, she manages simultaneously to lactate and negotiate killer deals. Cindy, a lovely mom I am sure, would be relegated to a small, "Nice Work If You Can Get It" type feature, right next to the story of Scrumptious, the toy poodle who rescued its comatose owner from a deadly house fire by beating him around the face and neck with a rawhide chew toy until he woke up.

The final element of any RJB session is, after having thoroughly lambasted your chosen victim, you then resurrect her in true Grrl Genius fashion. This assures that, in a sort of "karmic kareer" way, when you spectacularly fail in your current job, the universe will similarly resurrect you.

Now that we've cruelly eviscerated her, let's examine whether it is really Cindy's fault that she has been elevated by the press to be the most amazing mother since The Madonna, or for that matter, Madonna? Of course not. Cindy merely conceived a zygote and then bravely faced the adulation of the media. She is a Grrl Genius if she is willing to proclaim herself one.

Having mercilessly trampled women's magazine editors into the ground for presenting yet another idolized image of womanhood that no normal person can live up to without a platoon of servants and a squadron of stylists, can't we now agree that of course it is not their fault at all? The overworked, exhausted magazine editor is helpless in the face of the fact that their advertisers clamor to be part of supermodel gestation and delivery. These poor magazine editors are potential Grrl Geniuses, every last one of them.

My recreational-job-bashing session is now complete with the certain knowledge that although I would obviously do a better job than most magazine editors or reproducing supermodels, those people are blameless, as I will be the very next time I screw up.

GRRL GENIUS CAREER COPING TOOL #2:
Fantasy Fallback Jobs

In addition to berating the job performance of others, fantasizing about jobs I don't yet have is an important part of my Grrl Genius career strategy. The most important quality for any fantasy fallback job is that it be something that is considered "too difficult" to pick up later in life; the ideal fantasy fallback job should allegedly involve "talent" or "skills" that are supposedly out of the reach of "normal people." Well, Grrl Geniuses are not "normal people" so we are able to "think outside the cat box" when it comes to fallback careers in brain surgery or other supposedly "difficult" fields of endeavor.

—Prima Ballerina—

This has been my standard fantasy fall backjob ever since I began my study of ballet at the Mary Jane Olsen School of

Dance back in Roseville, Minnesota. Some people, bleating sheep who are content to follow the herd until they become little paper-bootied lamb chops, may feel that over thirty is way too late to begin a career as a prima ballerina. I don't let these naysayers hold me back, as I confidently stand in first position, noting my own excellent turnout. It's nice to know that if things don't work out in other areas, I can always fall back on my fouettés.

For those who need proof as to my obvious qualifications as a prima ballerina, you may note that my sister-in-law was a principal dancer with the Boston Ballet, and in a recent beachside bike ride, she became exhausted while I was still raring to go. Clearly, as ballet is a highly athletic endeavor, I am just hiding my balletic candle under a bushel by not hurling myself headlong into the world of professional dance.

Certain "friends" have tried to suggest to me that I am not being realistic, as they childishly accept the notion that worldwide dance fame involves a lot of dreary "training" and "practice." I suppose that might be true for certain types of prima ballerinas, but I intend to create a whole new art form. I will be a "naive ballerina," tossing aside all the weary, staid conventions, all that tiresome toe-balancing that has so crippled modern ballet, as I become the dance equivalent of Grandma Moses.

—Astronaut—

Astronaut is another fallback position I have mapped out. Although once I am firmly ensconced at NASA, I will insist on being called an "astrotrix" or "space gal," as the first, forgotten women in the U.S. space program were originally called.

Few people know that there were thirteen Grrl Genius pilots who passed the same rigorous flight tests as John Glenn and Alan Shepard. Apparently one of them, Jerrie Cobb, entered the program with twice as many air miles as John Glenn and emerged unscathed from a sensory-deprivation tank that had one of her male colleagues weeping and hallucinating that he was surrounded by barking dogs. Exhaustive testing showed that women astronauts were more able to resist radiation, heat, cold, pain, noise, and loneliness. Nevertheless, females were not initially allowed to go into space, unless you count a chimp named Glenda.

Difficulties for Grrl Geniuses in the space program have continued. As a budding "space gal," I was dismayed by the treatment of astronaut Shannon Lucid, who was in the Russian *Mir* space station for 188 days, by her cosmonaut colleagues, who said that they were happy to have her on the mission because they hoped she'd "tidy up the capsule."

When I heard this, I imagined myself having an astrotrix hissy fit and telling those cosmonauts, "I am an astronaut, get it? I am not your maid. I wasn't sent here to clean up the crumbs from your space-food sticks! You people can just make your own damn Tang as far as I'm concerned. And you might want to think about doing some laundry while you're at it, rinse out those nasty space suits of yours. It's been a while since they made the ones that could stand up on their own!"

As if this wasn't enough, Ms. Lucid's own family, upon greeting her at Cape Canaveral, reportedly asked her, "What's for dinner?"

"What's for dinner? What's for dinner?" I would reply as I angrily whipped off my helmet. "Perhaps you're unaware of the fact that I am a very busy astronaut! Did you know that there is not a Stop & Shop on the flaming reentry into the earth's atmosphere? I guess it must have slipped your mind that I've been in outer space for one hundred eighty-eight days, longer than anybody else at NASA, so here's a concept for you: Why don't we just freaking order out?"

Clearly, I have the necessary amount of "astro-sass" needed to get the job done. As for the alleged "scientific background" that everyone gets all worked up about, I figure I'll just bone up on all the "facts and figures" while I'm killing time in the sensory-deprivation tank. If multitasking isn't the hallmark of a true space explorer, I don't know what is.

—Higher Theoretical Physicist—

My other most favorite fantasy fallback job is that of higher theoretical physicist. Unfortunately, most people who get into the physics game waste too much of their valuable grant-earning years getting themselves an alphabet soup of fancy degrees. Not me. I realized one day while reading the *New York Times* science section that you certainly don't need to spend the big tuition money to get a handle on higher-theoretical physics. Not if you've just got a natural knack for it as I do.

For example, I read recently that some of my fellow physicists recently proved some old theory of Albert Einstein's called the cosmological constant. They did this by lounging around in their cushy offices, high in their ivory towers, and "observing" a bunch of supernovas in deep space (or so they claim). As a way to get more grant money, so they can continue "observing" and ordering expensive take-out meals, they've decided to announce the "fact" that the universe is not sitting still or imploding, but is in fact expanding rapidly under the pressure of a mysterious repulsive force, just like old Al (and most likely his wife, Mileva) said it was. Of course these "experts" don't have any interest in telling you what the mysterious repulsive force is, because that would obviously mean their scientific gravy train is pulling into the station.

With my natural flair for higher-theoretical physics, I figured out right away that the mysterious repulsive force that is causing the universe to expand can certainly be no other than noted big fat idiot Rush Limbaugh. End of story.

How is it that physics talent like mine is going unexploited and unfunded?

The beauty of the whole physics racket is the fact that physicists are always claiming to "prove" things, but very few people understand these supposed "proofs." Certainly not the bean counters in Washington who hand out all that sweet federal cash. These physics sharpies are laughing all the way to the bank as they feast on fine cabernet and government cheese, pawing through their kids' toy chests trying to find an action figure to name their next interstellar phenomenon after. It only takes a little cross-checking to figure out that Top Quark was a Hasbro toy long before it was a hard-to-find subatomic particle.

Believe you me, when I make my move, I'll happily send some champagne and caviar to the few eggheads who could try to bust up my beautiful physics scam, and we'll all knowingly wink and nod, as we toss back a toast to the government saps who eagerly await our next "discovery."

Once I get on the government science dole, I've got a lot of theories all ready and waiting. My current favorite is a variation on the brilliant "string theory" that those MIT jokers rode all the way to the Nobel bank. My theory is called the O's Theorem, which postulates that the entire universe burst forth from an infinitely small axis formed of pastalike circles not unlike those found in SpaghettiOs. It's an elegant theory that the think tankers are bound to eat up like, well, SpaghettiOs.

Once I'm the fair-haired grrl of higher-theoretical physics, no one will dare question my methods. No one will think of asking why it takes thousands of dollars in spa treatments to come up with one little theorem, and if they do, I'll just point out that whereas some geniuses need to sit in a think tank, I need to sit in a seventeen-jet, Swiss spa tub, thank you very much!

GRRL GENIUS CAREER COPING TOOL #3:
The "Really, Great, Wow" Method

Many Grrl Geniuses find themselves working in fields where grrls may still be in the minority. Since part of the guiding ethos of the whole Grrl Genius twelve-step program is the importance of not bashing potential Enlightened Males, the "Really, Great, Wow" Method is an indispensable tool.

Oftentimes, potential Enlightened Males have not been raised to think of the opposite sex as their intellectual equals any more than they have been raised to think of the family dog as their equal. This sometimes results in their overpraising their female colleagues, giving out compliments as if they were dog biscuits, amazed that someone handicapped with two X chromosomes can manage to perform the same tasks they accomplish using the standard X and Y chromosome combo platter.

When interviewing Grrl Genius job candidates, a potential Enlightened Male sometimes panics, automatically lapsing into what I call "default dating behavior." In his confusion, he tries to impress the Grrl Genius job candidate with *his* qualifications and amazing achievements, instead of vetting hers.

An easy way out of this sticky situation is simply for a Grrl Genius to limit her responses to three words: "Really?" "Great!" and "Wow!" It's important not to embellish these responses, as they have been thoroughly lab-tested by me on countless interviews, and I know for a fact that saying "Oh, really?" or "That's great!" simply dilutes the result. Don't think that they are too corny or over-the-top, because, trust me, these are the responses that work.

Once the interview has gotten to the "Really, Great, Wow" stage, it's important to stick to the program. I once interviewed for a highly paid television writing job and managed to say nothing but "Really, Great, Wow" for thirty-seven full minutes. Rather than bore my bosses-to-be with a lot of pesky information about my achievements or personality assets, I simply became a "good date," eagerly admiring their personalities and achievements. Impressive they were too. Among other things I was thrilled to learn was that one of them even drove a Porsche! Unfortunately, during my thirty-seven minutes of "Really, Great, Wow" I learned some tragic details about the trials of Porsche ownership. Silently, I vowed to do what I could to help, perhaps send a letter to Jerry Lewis, asking him to lose those whining cripples he's always shilling for and instead raise money for middle-aged men who are trapped in the senseless nightmare that is German-sports-car maintenance.

Needless to say, I got the job.

"Really?" you may ask, as a nascent Grrl Genius.

In response, I would nod knowingly, to which you would wisely respond, "Great! Wow!"

GRRL GENIUS CAREER COPING TOOL #4:

Try Anything Once

This Grrl Genius career tool is one of the most important because it effectively validates all of my schizophrenically random career choices. Without this essential tool, I could be seen as a shiftless dilettante, incapable of focusing or achieving on any sustained basis. With this tool in my little pink handbag, I become a multitalented Renaissance woman, the essence of Grrl Genius careerdom.

From foot modeling to strawberry picking, from jingle singing to writing jokes for a celebrity yogi to being paid to play R-rated practical jokes on strangers, the more bizarre the job, the more it is just another feather in my Grrl Genius hat.

A perfect example of my willingness to "try anything once" happened when a commercial agent called me in the not so distant past with a job audition for a print ad. The ad was part of a "Jockey for Her" campaign, and they wanted actual television writers and producers to be photographed standing around in their panties.

"Jockey for Her" had already done a successful ad just like this with real women doctors. In the ad, the women are standing there, looking at EKG strips, or sizing up tumors in a specimen pan trying to figure out what size fruit they most closely resemble. These dedicated lady doctors are so absorbed in the tricky business of saving lives that they don't even notice that someone has pulled down their pants.

Hey, it can happen.

In the ad I was auditioning for, I would be busy trying to write a joke on some sitcom. As usual, it would revolve around the horny grandma on the show who keeps trying to join the volunteer fire department. The joke would feature a lot of hunky fireman extras, and the hilarious punch line would undoubtedly feature a big brass pole. I would be so busy slaving over my hot joke that I wouldn't even notice that my little plaid skirt was suddenly around my ankles. As this has happened more times than I care to think about, I felt sure that the ad would be both tasteful and realistic.

I obeyed my own Grrl Genius career advice and agreed to go to the audition, because I would try anything once. Another good reason to go was that I was fresh out of operating funds, and these people were willing to pay a lot of money for me to drop my drawers. Also, unlike most of the other "Can I look up your dress?" offers I receive, this one would involve a lot of airbrushing. Additionally, it would annoy my parents, which is always a nice bonus.

My agent told me to wear pants and a T-shirt and reminded me to wear underwear, which I usually make a point to remember whenever I'm planning on showing someone what my goddaughter refers to as "my bamma and my privacy."

When I got to the audition, they started rolling the camera and asked me about my television-writing career. I thought that it was great that they wanted to know me as a writer, that I wasn't just another literary piece of ass to them. As it happened, I had a big network pitch coming up at NBC. They wanted to hear all about it, so I figured, hey, I would try it out on them, just for practice.

I started pitching the show, a young woman who leaves the big city to return home to help run the family funeral parlor, where she learns week after week that life is, after all, for the living. The underwear people were loving it, laughing and crying in all the right places. I was right in the middle of the pitch when the casting director, teary-eyed with laughter, suddenly said, "Oh my God, that was so brilliant that I totally forgot to ask you to take your shirt off!"

I admit it, I was shocked. Because as I understood it, we were here to evaluate my butt, not my tits. I'm not that in love with either area, but I'm approximately one thousand times more likely to show you my rear end than my boobs. I don't really know why, it just seems to me that showing my butt seems defiant, in a "kiss my ass" kind of way, whereas girls who whip off their tops just seem trashy and pathetic. For example, I would never be caught dead working at Hooters, but I wouldn't mind working at Big Ass Nancy's, if there were such a place.

Since I had agreed to go on the audition, I felt as if I couldn't get out of it. Besides, I didn't want to violate one of my own Grrl Genius prime directives. I stood there red-faced, like a teenager way over her head in a strip poker game, and took off my shirt. As I did, they asked me to keep pitching the pilot because they couldn't "wait to hear the end of the story."

I tried to tell myself I was like Scheherazade. Except that instead of wearing shimmering veils, I spun my tales in a tattered, frayed, used-to-be-pink bra that was now the gray-pink color of old bubble gum under a school desk. So I stood there in that bad bra and pitched a pilot, in my underwear. The titty-casting people kept laughing, but I didn't know anymore if they were real laughs or if they were just "we feel so sorry for you in that sad gray bra" laughs. They told me that they were sure the TV show would get made and would become a big hit. They were excited that they'd be able to say they "knew me when." Yes, they knew me when I stood in a terrible bra, under fluorescent light, and allowed myself to be filmed trying to sell a TV series.

A week later, wearing a good bra, I pitched the show at NBC. They hated it. I briefly considered taking off my shirt, but didn't think it would help. I wanted to tell those shortsighted fools at the network how wrong they were, how the "Jugs Judges" had hung on my every word. Unfortunately, the truth was that as much as the jugs people had loved my TV show, I had to admit that they really weren't that into my jugs because I didn't get the titty job either.

Now, the importance of this potentially depressing story is not whether I "succeeded" or "failed" as either a writer or as a piece of sweater meat. The issue is not whether I have a nimble mind or a nice rack. You can't get distracted by the whole IQ-versus-cup-size debate. The crucial thing to take away from this is that I was willing to try anything once. That is the lesson to be learned here. Why is this a good thing? Because I say it is, and that's enough for me.

If you don't like that, an alternative lesson could be that there is a huge investment opportunity waiting in franchising Big Ass Nancy's, coming soon to a local mini-mall near you.

The most important thing I learned was that my mother was not kidding around when she stressed the importance of wearing clean underwear. Clearly, your Grrl Genius career could depend on it.

Grrl Genius Career Coping Tool #5:

Getting Revenge

Obviously this is a career tool that should be reserved for special occasions. The possibility of seeking revenge is something that should be held in reserve, like a fine vintage wine. You must trust me on this. The Xerox (Michon) of your boss's ass that she made when she was really drunk at the Christmas party will only improve with age.

It's important to note that the whole Grrl Genius program is based on personal responsibility, recognizing your
own genius and being supportive of the genius of others.

But sometimes, some people just push it too far.

That's when a Grrl Genius, for the good of all, must
get revenge. Perhaps the most perfect example of Grrl
Genius job revenge that I have ever heard was deftly carried
out by my Grrl Genius cousin Jen, when she was working
as a waitress at a seafood restaurant in a wealthy Virginia
college town.

It was a warm spring night, and everyone in the small
town had their drinking pants on. Due to the beginning of
finals, the restaurant—I don't remember the name, but it
was something both naughty and nautical like Cap'n Thar
She Blows—was having an extended, six-hour happy hour,
more like a happy day. They were serving up flagons of ale
for twenty-five cents, and schooner-sized margaritas for a
dollar.

In addition to the whole "shave his belly with a rusty
razor" ambience of the place, the waitresses, Jen included,
were forced to dress in full serving-wench drag, complete
with a short, poufy skirt and a ridiculous white, lace-up
bustier that served your breasts up so high that on long
nights they made an excellent chin rest.

Since it was the end of the school year, most of the wait-
staff had quit, so Jen was forced to work the entire outer
deck by herself. There was one bartender, one blender,
and a lot of people ordering dollar margaritas. The situation was obvious to everyone except one table of three
sorority sisters, who seemed to feel that Jen was not being
an efficient-enough serving wench. One of the sisters, let's
call her Muffy, grabbed Jen with her perfectly French-
manicured talons, thus breaking the cardinal rule of food
service: never, *ever*, grab your server.

Muffy: *Excuse me!* Hello! We ordered more margaritas?

Jen: I know, and the thing is, so has everyone else, and there's one bartender, one waitress, and one blender. So I'm sure you can see the problem.

Muffy: Y'all don't get it. I don't care about the problem. This is just completely ridiculous, we've been waiting for, like, ever!

Jen: Since it's obvious that you seem to require a pretty constant dosage of margaritas, the only thing I can suggest is that you order your next round earlier.

Muffy: That is, like, so retarded!

Jen: I'm sorry, it's, like, all I can do.

Muffy: Are you, like, making fun of me?

Jen: No. I would, like, never do that.

The sorority sisters continued to hassle Jen throughout the evening, constantly grabbing at her and belligerently demanding speedier booze delivery. After last call, they insisted on getting three separate checks, and each of them paid the bill exactly, to the penny, leaving no tip.

Jen was incensed and followed them out into the parking lot. Shakily, she told them off. She told them that they had been rude and inconsiderate throughout the evening, and that she was a good waitress, who was trying her best, and that she had never been stiffed for a tip in her life.

The sorority sisters just laughed, and one of them said, "Well, I guess there's, like, a first time for everything!" Then they threw a single dollar bill at Jen, and got into their BMW.

As they squealed off, Jen stood there, humiliated, angry and tired. She dejectedly rested her chin on her breasts and was about to begin sobbing when she realized something.

They had each paid their bill with a personal check.

They had each paid with a personal check that revealed

their address, their phone number, their bank account number, and their social security number.

Did Jen get revenge? Of course, but what's important is the particular, Grrl Geniusy nature of her revenge. She didn't mess up their credit or trash their cars or make obscene phone calls, because that is not the Grrl Genius way. What she did wasn't illegal, and if forced to testify in a court of law, she could truthfully say that what she did should be construed as being helpful, humanitarian even.

She simply ripped out an ad from a magazine for some important information. She simply filled out the convenient response card, thereby making sure that each of the nontipping sorority sisters was signed up to receive that helpful, free information.

For a new herpes medication.

Due to the practice of selling names on mailing lists, each of those charming young Greek ladies soon received a deluge of mail at the sorority house. Big, colorful solicitations that began "Dear Syphilis Sufferer" or "Genital Warts Are No Fun!" or "Be Rid of Your Chancres Forever!"

Jen heard through the grapevine that the three weird sisters were nearly apoplectic about their constant crotch-rot mailings, and of course the more they denied it, the guiltier they sounded.

It makes me happy to know that, due to the perniciousness of direct-mail companies, even now, somewhere, a former sorority sister named Muffy or Ditsy or Buffy is angrily denying the obvious truth. The obvious, embarrassing truth that has become apparent to everyone in her household, due to the daily flood of letters that excitedly inform Bitsy of all the new ways to get rid of the open, weeping sores that cover her most private parts. I can hear her even now saying:

"I, like, don't even know what genital crabs look like!"

Oh yes, my cousin Jen is a Grrl Genius.

A GRRL GENIUS FACTETTE

Alanis Morissette's *Jagged Little Pill* has outsold any of the albums released by the Beatles.

The Dawn of Grrl Genius:

Grrl Chimp

Primordial
Ooze
(excellent facial
masque)

Cro Grrldon

Neandergrrl

A Pictorial History of the Ascent of Grrl Genius

Grrlstralopithecus

Grrl Ganthropus

Grrl Genius

A GRRL GENIUS LITTLE PINK POST-IT

....

Hey, Grrl Genius!

So your boss stole your good idea at work today, so what. It was midnight, and you were in the writers' room on that crummy sitcom you work for. One more joke and everyone could go home. All of a sudden it came to you, the perfect joke, and you said it. Your boss, the one who thinks that women can't be smart or funny, looked at you, horrified, because he knew it was the perfect joke. Then, suddenly, an evil Grinchy smile came over his face. He looked you straight in the eye and said, "You know what, you read my mind."

You read his mind. Because to him, it was more acceptable that you were a sorceress with magical powers than it was that you were both smart and funny. He is so sure that you have to be a man to have a good idea. Clearly, he is not an Enlightened Male.

What he obviously doesn't know is that the word *idea* itself literally means "inner-female muse"; it comes from the Greek root *eide*. In numerous cultures in the ancient world there were goddesses or muses—for example, Shakti, Psyche, and Sophia—who were said to be the source of all ideas. In ancient cultures, the mysterious conception of a new idea was linked to the mysterious conception of a new human being, and both these processes were considered "feminine" in nature. In other words, ideas are a "Grrl thing."

What you need to remember, Grrl Genius, is that he can try to steal your idea, but he can never steal the "idea of idea." Besides, now that you are on the path of Grrl Geniushood, who is to say that you aren't a magical sorceress as well?

Step Six

"Made a Decision to Love Our Grrl Genius Good Looks"

I don't look like a model and that's okay with me,
because I don't want to look like a whippet or
any other shaky dog.

—KAREN KILGARIFF

I never worry about diets. The only carrots that interest
me are the number you get in a diamond.

—MAE WEST

What is beautiful is good,
and who is good will soon be beautiful.

—SAPPHO

I'm just a person trapped inside a woman's body.

—ELAYNE BOOSLER

—Hair—

Over her lifetime, the average American woman spends more money for what she puts on her head (hair care, makeup, skin creams, etc.) than what she puts in her head (higher education, books, periodicals).

If the average American woman took the same amount of money she spends on her hair alone and spent it on intellectual improvement, she would have . . . well, in my opinion, she'd probably have really bad hair.

The first creature to love me obsessively for how I looked was my best friend Denise Steiner's talking pet crow, Casey. The Steiners were a groovy Catholic family across the street who had liberal thoughts on child rearing and many weird pets. In addition to the crow, they had a lizard, a monkey, and a poodle. Jim and Joe Steiner, the older boys in the family, were sullen and scary. They had a rock band called the Epilogue of Total Destruction. Not until many years later did I realize that the band's name was a paradox: How could there be an epilogue of total destruction? I mean, if everything is destroyed, who exactly is going to write that epilogue?

The point of the band was not to debate the nonmeaning of its name. Since the point of the band was to get high and get laid, the actual epilogue of the now-defunct Epilogue of Total Destruction would only need to be two words long: "Mission accomplished."

Casey the talking crow was the mascot of the band, and he lived in the Steiners' backyard in a swinging bachelor nest that he decorated with whatever shiny, flashy objects caught his beady little black eye. Every morning, the crow would fly up to Jim and Joe's window and screech, "Jim! Joe! Up!" I'm not sure who exactly taught the crow to talk, but I know the Steiners were devoted fans of the *Hollywood Squares,* so it shouldn't have been a surprise that the crow sounded like an eerie combination of Charles Nelson Reilly and Paul Lynde with maybe a touch of Jim J. Bullock thrown in.

In those days, I still had natural-blond hair. Apparently Casey would not be satisfied until he made my every golden hair on my head his. He would fly over me as I walked to school, dive-bombing me from above, batting me on the head with his enormous black wing and screaming, "I love you! I love you!" This went on for days, until he eventually knocked me flat into a snowbank with the force of his ardor.

Although I was terrified, a part of me was secretly thrilled. I, like all women who are loved only for their appearance, knew this love was false, but it was thrilling just the same. I hated the sharp pecks on my scalp, the dull thud of his heavy-winged bitch slaps, but I loved the intensity of his passion. I resolved never to tell anyone of this forbidden feathered obsession, like the woman with a split lip who claims she only "fell down the stairs."

I also knew that his love would kill me. Rather than reveal our secret, I decided never to go to school again. Finally, after days of my faking sick, my parents interrogated me, and eventually I cracked. I told them of Casey's destructive love for me, and they told me to get over it. It was a conversation that, with endless cast changes, would be repeated many times in the future.

The next day, as I walked to school, as I looked up into Casey's favorite maple tree, the launchpad of his airborne love raids, there was no Casey. Not that day, or the next, or the next.

The Steiners were distraught. They put out all of Casey's favorite foods, his sardines and his braunschweiger, but the crow was nowhere to be seen. The whole family was despondent; the Epilogue of Total Destruction was now sadly mute. The family mourned in silence as the voice of Secret Square Paul Lynde echoed through the rec room, now seeming like just a pale imitation of Casey, his own feathered imitator.

Casey never came back. I was sure that it was my fault, like all small children who believe they are powerful.

Actually, it turns out that I was right. After I told my parents of the crow's interspecies infatuation, my dad complained about "that goddamned horny crow" to our well-armed neighbor Mr. Steincamp, who promptly shot him dead.

What did I learn from becoming the unwilling executioner of my best friend's beloved pet? I should have learned about the tragedy of love that can never be fulfilled. I should have learned that love needs to be based on mutual respect, and deep and abiding friendship, not to mention that love works out so much better when everybody is, at the very least, a mammal.

But what I learned is that being blond is a good way to get attention. I learned that frost and tip caps are better than Sun-In, that foils are better than caps, and that no-peroxide balliage is best of all.

Casey taught me the importance of stockpiling hair-coloring, so that in case of nuclear war I would still be forced to deal with the end of life as we know it, but at least I would not have to worry about dark roots.

I know, in my heart, that Casey would love the subtle three-toned honey blond of my totally artificial hair today. Casey would understand, as everyone should, that there are no natural adult blondes, that blondness is a calling. Casey would respect the sacrifices this blondness requires.

If I am quiet, I can still hear the echoes of Casey's voice, sounding like a blend of the voices of every popular closeted homosexual of the seventies. As his flamboyant cries of "I love you! I love you!" ring in my mind, my scalp tingles with the sense memory of how he tried to rip the flaxen strands out of my tender, small head to line his—well, per-

haps our—love nest. I do feel guilty sometimes, guilty that I
am the one who unknowingly signed his death warrant.

I especially feel the guilt when I am watching *Jeopardy*.
Jeopardy is a show where, if you watch it often enough, you
soon realize that the writers like to use certain answers over
and over. Every so often, when I am watching *Jeopardy*, a
white-hot pang of guilt shoots through me when that familiar $200 answer is given under the category of "Bird
Groupings," and I am reluctantly forced to whisper the
question "What is a murder of crows?"

I still obsess about my hair, and I suppose I always will.
As a Grrl Genius I have finally accepted that what's inside
my head is more important than what grows out of it, but I
feel that it is part of my genius to love both my brain and
the faked-up flaxen hair that grows on top of it.

—*Face*—

The business of facial beauty, skin care, makeup, and plastic surgery is responsible for $22 billion in revenue annu-
ally.

Female insecurity about looks begins early. In a survey
of elementary-school girls, they were asked to name who
was the most unattractive girl in their class, and six out of
ten girls said, "Me." That is a truly horrifying statistic. Six
out of ten girls in this country don't just think they're ugly,
they think they are the ugliest.

The bold red letters read, "Human Eyes in Glass Jars."
I am in the Minneapolis–St. Paul International Airport,
waiting in the check-in line. I am standing behind a tall,
dangerous-looking man in full Unibomber drag, a look I
find impossibly sexy. It's the look of a perpetual bad boy
that just screams, "With your good lovin', you could fix
me." People are carrying boom boxes and golf bags and

backpacks, and the tall guy has this big white box that says on it, "Human Eyes in Glass Jars." Just looking at the box, I become physically ill and have to sit down on my Samsonite.

Why does the box have to be so specific? Why does the box insist, like an endlessly chatty aunt who gives you the intimate details of her acid reflux, on telling you way more than you want to know? Why can't the box just say "Caution: Medical Materials" or even something whimsical like "Jeepers Creepers Peepers" or just a simple "Eyeballs R Us"? Why does the box force me to imagine the eyeballs, blue and green and hazel, rolling around like so many pimiento-stuffed martini olives inside glass jars?

But then I'm sensitive about eyeballs, since I once had mine briefly removed, while I was awake to, for lack of a better term, watch the whole thing as it happened.

When I was a seventeen-year-old freshman at Northwestern University, I got very sick. I had been at school all of three weeks. At the time, I lived in a coed dorm suite with three other girls. The boys on our side of the floor had, with their rapier-sharp wit, nicknamed us "Tits," "Legs," "Ass," and "The Black Girl." Much as I would have enjoyed the change of pace of being "The Black Girl," I was "Ass."

Because I was a major musical-comedy victim, I was constantly running around campus in spandex and leg warmers and the flimsy, ripped sweatshirts made fashionable by the hit welding movie *Flashdance.* When I got cast in the big musical revue directed and choreographed by the top musical-comedy queen in the theater department, it was the biggest thing that had ever happened to me. "What a Feeling" only begins to describe how great I felt.

Two days into rehearsals, when I got a sore throat, I felt my gorgeous jazz-hands musical-comedy world crashing around me, and I ran off to the student health center, where I was told I could get free cough drops. I went to get the cough drops and they put me through a three-day battery of tests, which seemed like a lot of fuss just for some Halls Mentholyptus. Finally, they sat me down and told me that I had a serious case of Graves' disease, which is a goddamned pessimistic name for a disease and not a very nice thing to hear.

So now I was sick, I had a goiter the size of my fist, and the medicine they gave me didn't do squat. I just kept getting worse. So they gave me more tests, and I went to hospital after hospital, with my dad finally dragging me to some famous clinic where they said they would like to do some exploratory brain surgery and I said I didn't want exploratory brain surgery, I just came for the free cough drops, and from now on I was buying my own. There is no free lunch and there are no free cough drops. Lesson learned, case closed.

Except the case wasn't closed, because I had started to get the facial disfigurement that accompanies Graves' disease, the exophthalmos of the eyes, which means that your eyeballs are being slowly pressed out of their sockets. It is the look that made Marty Feldman famous, but I had a feeling it would not have the same effect on my career.

The first thing they did was to give me radiation. I had to drink the radiation. I had to go to the hospital and sit in a lead room, where a guy in a space suit handed me a lovely radiation beverage. I remember thinking, "If he has to wear that getup just to carry the beverage, should I really be drinking the beverage?" But then he double-dog-dared me to drink it, so of course I did.

After the radiation came the four plastic reconstructive surgeries. My doctor was a highly skilled German man with the artistic sensibility of Matisse and the bedside manner of Mengele. My surgeon liked to have his patients awake when he sliced up their heads; he said that was because he was rebuilding the muscular structure of the eye, he liked everything to be alert and twitching. Yummy.

Let me just say this about the surgeries, there are many good reasons why people are usually asleep during surgery, and if they ever give you a choice between awake and asleep, I give a hearty thumbs-up to asleep.

The beauty of the face is so subjective. Back in Roseville, my next-door neighbor Kathy Amerongen was the most exotically beautiful girl I had ever seen. She was six years older than me and was our baby-sitter. The source of her beauty was the giant metal neck brace that she wore night and day to correct her scoliosis. The brace consisted of giant, shiny metal bars that encircled her entire torso, crowned by a lovely pale Naugahyde chin rest that cradled her delicate, unblemished chin. To me, with her perfect posture and fantastic paraphernalia, she looked like some kind of outer-space superheroine. Like a small Ubangi child who can't imagine its mother without a ten-inch plate forced into her lip, I couldn't imagine Kathy without her brace; it was an integral part of her allure.

Later, I realized that it was Kathy's sassy, surly Grrl Genius attitude that made me think the brace was merely an elaborate fashion accessory. Because she was such a natural diva, anything she did would have seemed cool. Because of Kathy and her iron maiden we won tickets to the local amusement park for having the most successful muscular dystrophy backyard carnival in our district. As we went door-to-door, shilling for noted cripple pimp Jerry Lewis, there wasn't a single person who refused to buy a raffle ticket from the girl who was so obviously one of "Jerry's kids."

I was thinking about Kathy Amerongen as I lay in my bed in Michael Reese hospital, my eyelids sewn shut for a Jesus-esque three days after my eye surgery. I had stupidly told my parents not to come, and the only person I had to take care of me was my brusque German boyfriend whom I'd meant to break up with, but somehow hadn't gotten around to it. He was yet another bad boy whom I was sure I could fix with my good lovin'.

There were three more surgeries after that one. Most of the time I looked pretty bad. I was surprised that people used to come up to me on the El, total strangers, and say, "What happened to your face?"

Inside my head, I had a sassy diva, my inner Kathy Amerongen, who would snap back, "You wanna know what happened to my face? Okay, fine, but I'd like to know what happened to your freaking manners."

Why it is that people feel that your looks, good or bad, are any of their business? I can't even count the number of times I have been walking down the street, and some guy, a total stranger, will say to me, "Why don't you smile, you'll look so much prettier if you smile." My inner Kathy Amerongen always wants to spit back, "Why don't you get hard, you'll look so much more useful if you have an erection." Of course, the real me never has the nerve to say it.

It is a well-known scientific fact that people think better of people who are good-looking. Juries, including the one that freed O. J. Simpson, are more likely to believe a good-looking defendant. Even babies, who haven't been influenced by fashion magazines, those slam books for grown-ups, will smile more when they look at pictures of traditionally "pretty faces."

Eventually, my face got fixed. When they rebuilt my eyes, they used donated human sclera, or dead-guy-eyeball stuff as I know it. Ever since the surgeries I just can't get enough of those corny stories about people who have donated dead-people stuff in them. The stories are always in magazines like *Woman's Day or Family Circle,* right next to a recipe for a Jell-O mold in the shape of the United States that is perfect for a

Fourth of July picnic. The stories are usually about people who get heart transplants and then start to take on the personality of the donor. Vegetarians who suddenly crave Chicken McNuggets, white-militia guys who suddenly "get" jazz.

Whoever donated my dead-guy-eyeball stuff (I always assume it was a man, I have no idea why) must have been a real wimp. Because my dead-eyeball guy cries at anything. He even cries at that Campbell's soup ad where the divorce-victim children try to get their parents, who are dating, to marry them all up into a Brady Bunch by making that really cruddy chicken-mushroom-soup casserole. My weenie dead guy cries his fool eyeballs out at that one, and I'm the one that's left sitting there looking like an idiot.

What, I wonder, is the etiquette on donated human parts? For example, can I be an eyeball donor myself, or is that tacky, like rewrapping a Christmas present and giving it to someone else? I mean, is my eyeball now just a used eyeball, or is it considered more like a classic eyeball, like a really cherry collectible eyeball?

I make fun of my pantywaist dead-eyeball guy, but the truth is, I love him. I think about how much I love him as the devilishly attractive Unibomber wanna-be loads his "Human Eyes in Glass Jars" onto the airport luggage conveyor belt. How can I ever thank my dead-eyeball guy for giving me my face back? I wonder. Both me and dead-eyeball guy get all misty and teary-eyed at the very profound thought that I can't, I can't thank him, except by being grateful. All I can do is treat me, and my sad-sack, weepy dead-eyeball guy to a martini, no olives, at the airport bar.

—*Body*—

In a recent survey, 31 percent of nine-year-old girls thought they were "too fat," and by age ten, 81 percent described themselves as "dieters."

In 1973 the word *cellulite* was imported into the United States by *Vogue* magazine, which described it as a "condition," a "disfiguring" texture of flesh that was "polluted with toxins." Prior to this date, cellulite was simply seen for what it is, normal, healthy female flesh.

On June 27, 2000, I ate a double-dip ice cream cone in my bikini, on the back deck. My bikini has push-up pads that make me feel better about my small breasts. Some of the ice cream dribbled onto my so-called cellulite, and I just licked it right off my own thigh. It was delicious.

Nancy Schmaedeke and I sat in Mary Jane Olsen's dance studio in Roseville, Minnesota, painted up like two-dollar whores. I studied dance with Mary Jane and her daughter Candy, and I also studied at the Children's Academy of Dramatic Arts with my impossibly named acting teacher Gloria Swenson.

Nancy and I watched as Candy Olsen demonstrated one last time the Annie Oakley tap number "You Can't Get a Man with a Gun." Maybe you can't, but if you could get a man with a gun, my guess it would be with the glow in the dark green fluorescent ruffles our parents were forced to buy for our recital, because they were fantastic. I watched Candy as she danced; I watched how her thighs rhythmically jiggled as she tapped away, and I wished that someday I would have that same pendulous shank of flesh hanging off my own thighs. Little did I know that one day I would, and that I would then proceed to waste entire decades of my life obsessing over it.

I "worry," like the horrifyingly vast majority of American women, about my weight. In a recent survey, 85 percent of women said that the number one thing they would wish for would be to lose ten or fifteen pounds. They would rather lose ten or fifteen pounds than receive a significant promotion at work or have a fulfilling love relationship.

No statistics were given as to whether they would be willing to mug an old woman or euthanatize a small puppy to achieve the desired weight loss.

According to actuarial tables, I am of average or below average weight for my height. According to me, I "feel" fat. Accordingly, I have done time in The Zone, I have gone on the high-fiber diet, the low-carbohydrate diet, the high-complex-carbohydrate diet, the yeast-free, gluten-free diet, the "caveman" diet, the Mediterranean diet, the sugar-busters diet, and the potatoes-not-Prozac diet. I have ingested the dried exoskeletons of dead sea creatures to absorb fat; I have taken fistfuls of supplements; I have drunk water from liter bottles and peed so frequently that I can't believe I didn't earn a salary for urinating, since on many days it was the most productive thing I did; I have eaten pineapple because it is a "miracle food"; I have eaten strawberries because their high fiber content makes them so difficult to digest that it actually takes more calories for your body to process them than they contain.

My wacky turban-wearing yoga teacher once told me that she was in favor of a nutritional system called UT, or urine therapy. According to this plan, you drink two ounces of your morning urine every day. Naturally, I found this repulsive. Then she told me it gets rid of cellulite, and I started considering it. I thought, you know, I could just put it in some really strong coffee or something. I am notoriously picky about food and beverages. Normally you couldn't pay me to put Mocha Mix in my coffee, but here I was, seriously considering whipping up a Decaf, No Foam, Pee Pee Latte to start off the day.

I have been tested for food allergies. I have given up meat; I have given up wheat; I have given up dairy; and I have come crawling back to all three. I once gave up sugar in any form including fruit, and that first night of sugar sobriety, I had a vivid dream that I was cradling an M&M the size of a small infant in my arms. In the dream I cooed and rocked that M&M and just licked it for hours.

I have unnecessarily tortured thousands of helpless food-service workers with requests for food to be steamed, not sautéed; for light oil, no oil; for the milk to be skim; for the meat to be white; and for all dressings, sauces, and condiments to please be served "on the side." I once wept openly because I found out that olives contain up to a hundred calories each due to their high fat content. I wept bitter tears for all the olives that I had eaten just to be polite, because I don't particularly like them.

I once contracted dysentery in a third-world country. Although I was miserable, secretly I was thrilled that at least I was losing weight. I have ordered sushi in less than sparkling-clean Japanese restaurants, secretly hoping that I might get a much-coveted tapeworm.

I have calculated how many calories I was burning while running, riding my bike, or swimming in the ocean and done the accounting necessary to work off an upcoming ice cream cone. I have even calculated the amount of calories burned off during a vigorous round of sex, remembering to include that the average amount of male ejaculate ingested orally is roughly equal to thirty calories, the same as a Hershey's Kiss. If the ejaculate ends up in any other orifice, it's 100 percent calorie-free. If you name any given food, I can more than likely tell you the exact calorie amount per serving, as well as the approximate fiber, sugar, and fat content, as well as where it rates on the glycemic index.

I have done seaweed wraps and mud baths and steam baths and have worn plastic pants to dance class. I bought the miracle thigh cream and I once FedExed my own feces to a nutritionist in Santa Fe. All I could think of is what a terrible job his poor receptionist had, sitting there all day and signing for poo.

However, because I have never forced myself to vomit, abused laxatives, been dangerously overweight or underweight (I wish), I am not considered to have an eating disorder.

Sadly, I am considered normal.

No man that I care about has ever called me fat. No man who has been intimate with me has ever said my thighs and ass were anything but scrumptious, nor have any of them ever said that what I consider to be my absurdly small breasts were anything but delectable morsels. It was not men who did this to me, who made me have such contempt for my body. I do this to me, ably guided by the thousands of ridiculous images that assault me daily from television, the movies, billboards, and fashion magazines.

I live in Los Angeles, home of the *Baywatch* ideal of beauty. It is important to note that *Baywatch* is the most watched television show on the planet. More people have seen *Baywatch* than have read Jane Austen. A few years ago, when a friend and I wrote a humor book about Jane Austen, I met with a studio executive about a TV project. My agent had told her about the book, and she eagerly asked me about it, wanting to know, "What is it like to work with Jane Austen?" I didn't have the heart to tell her that she was currently dead, so I just said, "She didn't give me any trouble." This woman, a graduate of a major university, had no idea that Jane Austen, although at the moment very popular in Hollywood, had been dead for more than 150 years. She didn't know that Jane Austen was a dead chick, but I'll bet she knew that *Baywatch* star Pamela Anderson Lee had removed her old implants and replaced them with newer, sportier sacs. In Los Angeles, that's what passes for valuable knowledge.

I have what have been politely referred to as ballerina breasts. Which would be great if they came with a ballerina ass, but apparently that is sold separately. My mother has fantastic knockers, and so do all my aunts. I remember that in junior high a friend's brother nominated me to be a member of The Itty Bitty Titty Committee, and I am now chairwoman emerita.

I, like almost every barely B, have thought about breast implants. I've thought that they would make me feel better about myself. Then my friend Shaana died of breast cancer, she didn't have implants, but it spooked me just the same, and I thought maybe I'd leave my tits alone for a while. Instead, I settled for various high-tech brassieres. The Wonderbra, The Miracle Bra; if there had been a resurrection bra where you rolled away a stone and found hooters everlasting, I'd have bought it. For now I have decided against implants, although I reserve the right to change my mind.

At one point, I thought, if I'm getting these new mamma jammas, I want people to know that I spent the money for them. So maybe I will get four of them—two up, two down, that would be fancy. For once I'll wear a double-breasted blazer and not be guilty of false advertising. In Los Angeles, a town that loves a gimmick, I'll manage the impossible, I'll be different. I won't just be the "it" girl, I'll be the "four-tit" girl. Network presidents will send me large baskets of tiny muffins as they slavishly fawn over me.

Naturally, I will eventually be starring in my own television series. Perhaps I'll be serving up a quadruple helping of laughs in the riotous sitcom *Four's Company*, or maybe I'll be coming at you with all four barrels blazing in the gritty hour police drama *Jugs and Mugs*, or maybe my four tatas will cover the four corners of the globe as I anchor the hard-hitting newsmagazine *Rack Focus,* or maybe I'll get in on the game-show craze as the multiple-mammaried host of *Knockers Wild.* The possibilities are endless.

Or maybe I'll just skip the whole thing and settle for a clear, unobstructed mammogram.

Ever since I was sixteen years old, I have cursed the two little poochy bulges of fat that rest on my strong outer thighs. I believed everything I ate that was "bad" traveled directly to them. After hating them so desperately for all these years, I finally decided, since my life was falling apart anyway, to have a handsome doctor stick a small instrument into them and vacuum them away while I lay there, fully conscious, talking about how much we both loved Lou Reed. It was like a really pleasant lunch meeting, except that no food was served, and our reason for spending time together was so that he could suck the fat out of my ass.

Is it a good idea to make a decision about elective surgery when you are recently separated from your husband? Normally, people get new, radical haircuts when a relationship is in trouble. I just went a little further. Instead of cutting off my hair, I cut off my thighs.

Undergoing a surgical procedure in order to not despise my body may seem like a failure of the Grrl Genius philosophy, but it is not. If I could have loved my body in its natural state, well, then, yay for me, but after a while I just couldn't. And the simple fact is, I don't live in my natural state. I don't sleep in the trees, swinging from vines; I don't snag trout bare-handed from mountain streams or wipe my butt with mulberry leaves. I do all sorts of other unnatural things, and no one tries to make me feel guilty about it.

I told my adorable gay friend Michael that I was considering liposuction and he was horrified. He said, "I just don't see how you, a feminist, or a womanist, or whatever the hell it is you are—"

"A Grrl Genius," I interrupted.

"Fine, I don't see how as a Grrl Genius you could consider mutilating yourself that way, it's just unnatural."

"Oh, please, as if you're frigging Mother Nature," I said. It wasn't much of a comeback, but it really got Michael's panties in a twist.

"I'm not saying I'm Mother Nature," he said. "I'm just saying that you should love yourself the way you are, you're beautiful, just how God made you." Just then I snapped, the way I always do when someone drags God or Hitler into their side of the argument.

I leaned across the table and looked deep into his tinted-blue contact lenses. "How can you sit there, giving me that advice through your three-thousand-dollar veneered teeth, that you thought up out of your moussed, blow-dried head. You are a giant hypocrite because, if you may recall, you've already had cosmetic surgery."

"I have not!" he spat back.

"Oh yes, you have, you're circumcised. That's cosmetic surgery." I didn't have any firsthand experience with his bulbous man trumpet, but I could see right away that my lucky guess had hit pay dirt, right between his legs.

He shifted uncomfortably in his chair. "That doesn't count," he sputtered. "That was done without my consent." By this point, he knew he had lost the argument.

"But you're glad it was done, aren't you?"

He nodded weakly. I knew that he was glad because I knew that he considers turtlenecks unbearably gauche in any context.

I finally decided to have the lipo when I first separated from my husband, sleeping in the borrowed apartment of an out-of-town friend. I went to the doctor my TV-star friend recommended, a darkly handsome Englishman. My fat-sucking doctor is the perfect combination of Henry

Higgins, who was of course an upper-crusty Brit, and Pygmalion, who was of course a sculptor. I walked out of his beautiful wood-paneled office humming "I Could Have Danced All Night," and two days later I was back with a Lou Reed CD in my purse to play during the surgery.

If you are going to do something self-destructive, there is hands down no one better than Lou Reed to play you through it. I knew that what I was doing was self-destructive, but I figured, hey, I never did cocaine in the eighties and I don't smoke pot or anything else. As far as self-destruction goes, I figured I was long overdue.

The most amazing thing about the lipo is I can truly say I did it for me, as it has been eight weeks since I had it and not a soul has noticed. Not a single person has mentioned that I look any different. Not even my estranged husband has been able to tell the difference.

Even so, I like it. Now, when I ride my bike, I only think about riding my bike. I don't think about whether that four pounds of fat is riding on either side of my hips, because I know it's not. I know that it is sitting, a surprisingly garish golden yellow, in the bottom of a hazardous-waste disposal bin in the office of Dr. Henry Higgins. I know because I saw it. I said good-bye to it. I asked for a few minutes alone with my fat. I told my fat I was sorry that I had blamed so much on it for all these years. I told my fat that it wasn't responsible for the jobs I didn't get, the people who didn't like me, the marriage not going so well.

Now, when I am sitting on the beach, I no longer despise other women for winning the genetic lottery, for not having that particular four pounds of fat. And I no longer judge the women who have the courage to hang on to that four pounds, or any other pounds. I know that they are honoring nature's wish, they haven't "let themselves go," they are simply following the wisdom of genetics that tells their bodies to preserve that fat like the gold that it is, so that the survival of the species can be insured, so that babies can be conceived and nourished.

I know that it doesn't matter a good goddamn if they get the fat ripped from their bodies, probably no one will notice. So if it makes them feel as good as it makes me feel, well, then, let her rip, I say. It's their money and their body. My friend Stephanie Miller had lipo, on the air, as she broadcast her drive-time radio show, and it was one of the funniest things I ever heard. Janeane Garafalo, my generation's Joan of Arc in that she has courageously led the assault against the tyranny of artificial beauty, had a breast reduction. She said it was one of the best things she ever did for herself, and I back her on it.

I decided to tell everyone about my flab suckage because, in case anyone should notice my body in a positive way, I didn't want her to think that my thighs got this way from anything healthy. I realized that in the almost ten years I've been writing for television, I've never even heard of a TV character getting liposuction, even though almost every actress I know who works on television has had it. If they haven't, it's usually because they have trainers and masseuses and personal chefs on full-time thigh patrol. They are usually also forced to maintain a rigorous smoking schedule.

The point of all this is that we are supposed to have choices. If I want to buy ridiculous shoes or a ridiculous car or a ridiculous operation with my disposable income, well, then, who should stop me? No one, because that is the Grrl Genius way. The lipo was worth it because it has shut off this thigh hatred that has droned in my head like a bad Bee Gees song for all these years.

Sitting in my friend's borrowed apartment, watching the fluid drain out of my slightly thinner bruised thighs, I had a stunning revelation. While taking a lovely and relaxing drug called Vicodin, I had yet another vision, another revelation. I realized, all of a sudden, that I knew how to create sustainable economic prosperity and permanently eradicate war.

Yeah, sure, maybe it was the Vicodin talking, but the vision that came to me was potentially life-altering, on a global level. During my two-day postlipo Vicodin binge, I created "The Grrl Genius Economic Manifesto for Sustained Prosperity and World Peace." It is both simple and elegant, like all great leaps forward in global consciousness.

My theory goes something like this: America is currently experiencing the longest period of economic growth in our history. Why? Because we essentially stopped participating in the dead-end economy of the military-industrial complex. Since the war machine produces only means of destruction and ugly outfits, it doesn't create real economic growth. The economy of death never created true wealth. That has now been proven.

If we want to sustain this growth, we must get rid of our more insidious dead-end economy, the economy of self-loathing. Since the end of the Great Depression and the beginning of the modern advertising industry, marketers have been convinced that for people to desire consumer items, they must be made to feel inadequate and inferior. Buy this sports car, this face cream, this dessert topping, or else you are a giant loser. When it was revealed through market research that women make disproportionately more of these consumer-spending decisions, it was then quite logically decided that women must be made to feel disproportionately more inadequate.

Hence the rise of the supermodel. There are a little over 3 billion women on planet Earth, and eight of them are supermodels. No offense to those eight Grrls, God bless them, in fact, but they are true genetic freaks. While I sat tending to my liposuction wounds, I got on the Internet and discovered that there are approximately 3.5 million hermaphrodites on planet Earth. Therefore, I deduced that the average women is roughly 437,500 times more likely to look like a hermaphrodite than she is to look like a supermodel. Point is, don't feel bad about not looking like a supermodel, feel bad about not being a hermaphrodite, because at least you had a shot at that one.

After another Vicodin and some surprisingly guilt-free Krispy Kremes, I then had a further revelation. I realized who is paying the enormous price for our economy of inadequacy. Surprisingly, it is men. The simple fact is that male humans live seven years less than females. No other primates have this disparity. There is only one reason for it. Men have been tricked into working themselves into an early grave so they can try to compete for eight women. Heterosexual men, if left to their own sexual devices, could be blissfully happy with any yummy, squishy, rounded Grrl Genius that loves their throbbing, pulsing love wand. Yet, Madison Avenue has tricked them into believing they cannot function sexually unless their mate has done everything in her power to look like a genetic freak.

I now understood that this economy of self-loathing is literally killing the men, and it is making the Grrl Geniuses everywhere very cranky. I decided that it has got to go.

I realized that, like all paradigm shifts, there would be a cost to implementing "The Grrl Genius Economic Manifesto for Sustained Prosperity and World Peace." If people suddenly loved themselves and thought that their bodies were beautiful, there would be a transition period during which the economy would take a drastic downturn. People would stay home in droves, happily buying nothing and wearing nothing, except maybe some sweatpants if they got a chill. They would stay home and be shagging each other for days on end on the kitchen counter, in the rumpus room, in the Barcalounger.

Eventually, after this period of sweatpants and serious shagging, which I, as a Vicodin-enhanced Grrl Genius economist, saw as a necessary market correction, these people would emerge from their homes, smiling and contented, ready to buy sports cars and face creams and dessert toppings just for the fun of it. Instead of buying a Porsche because you feel sexually inadequate, you would now buy a Porsche because nothing tops off a good afternoon of shagging quite like slathering yourself with expensive face cream and dessert topping and driving around in a fast German sports car. This is my bold Grrl Genius vision for the new world order. Lots of shagging and then increased spending and production, followed by continued, sustained shagging for everyone. Whoever called economics the dismal science was not thinking about it from the Grrl Genius point of view.

Oh, yeah, and if everyone was getting laid, there would be no more war.

After the Vicodin wore off, and the bruises died down, I decided that my economic manifesto still made sense. The whole world would change if everybody loved the way he or she looked naked. If all the women in the world followed *only this step* of my twelve-step program, the world would be transformed for the better overnight.

For my manifesto to be implemented, everybody would need to think he or she was beautiful, the way a baby knows for sure that it's beautiful. My niece Maya Cathryn Michon knew she was beautiful from the moment she was born. She knew that every part of her, including the drool that dribbled out of her perfect lips, was splendid. Her piss was delightful, her boogers magnificent. She could spend hours staring at her impeccably formed hand, tenderly sucking and tasting each stunningly gorgeous dimpled finger, and who could blame her?

I decided to be part of the solution and not part of the problem. In completing this sixth step of the Grrl Genius program, by making a decision to love my Grrl Genius good looks, I have begun phase one of the implementation of "The Grrl Genius Economic Manifesto for Sustained Prosperity and World Peace."

I have decided that I am beautiful. Not because of the hair coloring or the reconstructive facial surgery or the lipo. There's nothing wrong with those things, but they are like scarves or shoes or bracelets, they are mere ornaments to my actual beauty. I am beautiful because I can do a handstand, because of the snorty, loud way I laugh at your jokes, because my lips are luscious and the back of my neck is irresistible, dotted as it is with a pale birthmark that serves as an X to mark the spot most worth kissing. I am beautiful because I can hilariously imitate almost anyone, because I have impossibly long eyelashes, because I have delicate ankles and fantastic toe cleavage, and because I look great in a hat. I am beautiful because I say I am. I'm beautiful because after all these years I finally decided just to believe it.

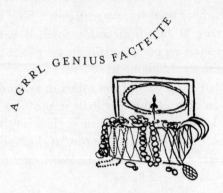

A GRRL GENIUS FACTETTE

In addition to ensuring the continuation of the human race, pregnancy can help you do splits!

Due to the hormone-induced loosening of soft joint tissue, which allows the pelvic bones to shift to accommodate the growing fetus, doing splits for the first time is much more likely when you are pregnant.

So if you always wanted to do splits, get knocked up!

A GRRL GENIUS LITTLE PINK POST-IT

Hey, Grrl Genius!

Did you know that the unique physical capabilities of the female brain are most ideally suited to life in the twenty-first century?

Brain functions that have traditionally been regarded as male, the aggressive hunting instinct, logical linear thought, reside in the left brain. Creative, nurturing, artistic, intuitive, and emotional functions are found in the right brain. Both men and women have these capabilities, but the part of the brain that connects these two halves, the corpus callosum is found to have 10 to 33 percent more neuronal fibers in Grrls.

What this means in a practical sense is that your average Grrl Genius brain is physically more capable of multitasking, using both the left and right sides of the brain. This a skill that is essential in the computer age. This multitasking function in female humans evolved over tens of thousands of years as women had to simultaneously nurse and care for infants, gather food, manage people, plant crops, etc. Men evolved as specialists, who only focused on tracking and killing prey. In modern society, having the kind of brain that can multiply process information is a better job skill than having the ability to completely shut off your right brain's emotions and use your left brain to go off and slay a wildebeest. Oh, sure, it comes up, just not that often.

This doesn't mean that Enlightened Males can't learn to switch back and forth from the left to right brain, it just means that they will have to work a little harder at it. Not that it's a contest, but it's important to note that there are still areas in which men retain undisputed superiority over women—lifting heavy stuff and pee-writing their name in the snow, for example.

After all, a Grrl Genius can't have everything.

Step Seven

"Made a Searching and Fearless Inventory of Our Sexuality and Embraced It!"

In my sex fantasy, nobody ever loves me for my mind.

—NORA EPHRON

Really, that little deelybob is too far away from the hole.
It should be built right in.

—LORETTA LYNN

I'm saving the bass player for Omaha.

—JANIS JOPLIN

Sex has ruined me. I can almost pinpoint the very day that it ruined me. I'm not exactly sure why, but my mother recently sent me a bunch of old papers, including a copy of my sixth-grade diary. According to this diary, I was involved in some very interesting projects: I was composing a full-length opera about the unfairness of my parents. I was also in the midst of teaching my two cats the power of human speech, a project that I felt quite sure would win me the Nobel Prize.

I kept detailed logs on my experiments, spending at least an hour a day with the cats, trying to get them to replicate tones and inflections. I would lean close into their little pink noses and say "Meow? Meow?" with the tone of my voice rising precipitously at the end. Sometimes they would reproduce the exact sound, although whether it was from a desire to learn English or from my holding firmly on to their tails to make them pay attention, it was hard to tell. I was sure that from our tonal exercises the cats would quickly progress to words and sentences.

Then, one day, my diary of opera lyrics and detailed scientific notes was interrupted by a fateful entry that took up an entire page but was only one sentence long.

"Eric Lindstrom is so cute."

That was the day sex ruined me. As estrogen began pumping through my veins, my eggs ripened, and my brain atrophied. I never finished the opera, my cats died without speaking a word of English, and I devoted years of my life to worshiping men, writing terrible poetry about them, dreaming of them, crying over them.

Sex does not ruin boys the way it can ruin Grrls. When boys become obsessed by sex, they try to achieve, to attract Grrls. Grrls know that boys don't care how smart or strong or successful you are, they care that you think *they* are strong and smart and successful. So Grrls start to act stupid, as many surveys have shown. Boys' balls drop and Grrl grades drop, almost overnight. Grrls also immediately become insecure about their looks.

On the other hand, boys, and the men they grow into, tend to overrate their attractiveness. Hence the common phenomenon of a guy with a gut the size of Montana and a belt buckle the size of a wide-screen TV hoisting his girth into a pickup truck with a "No Fat Chicks!" sticker on the bumper.

Hence the common phenomenon of supermodels "feeling fat."

So, like six out of ten of my classmates, I felt ugly and balanced this out by acting stupid. I put on a convincing stupid act throughout junior high and high school, pretending not to know things so as not to intimidate. By the time I became a National Merit Scholarship semifinalist and got my picture in the paper, it seemed like my cover had been busted. Rickie Overgaard, captain of the football team, stopped me in the hall the day after my picture was published.

"Hey, Duck!"

The nickname that ballet had earned me never failed to sting. I made the daily effort to walk pigeon-toed, which with my turnout equaled something like normal walking.

"What?" I said, feeling his eyes staring at my shiny-green-polyester-encased butt, not understanding that the stare was supposed to be a compliment.

"Hey, I saw your picture in the paper, with all the brains. What's the deal, you took, like, a test or something?"

"Oh, it was dumb."

"But you scored like a brain, what's up with that?"

I saw my social life flash before my eyes, then I leapt in for the save.

"I cheated."

A grin of approval filled his beefy face. "Cool."

Fortunately Rickie Overgaard was stupid enough to believe that you can cheat on the PSAT. With the help of the rumor mill and my flaky behavior, I was able to keep my intellect incognito until graduation. Of course, as you know, it wasn't until many years later, when I developed the Grrl Genius twelve-step program, that I fully "outed" myself as the genius I am.

Now, following my own program, I boldly take step seven and embrace my Grrl Genius sexuality. No longer do I write excruciating, poorly spelled lust poetry, like this little gem I composed for Eric Lindstrom, back in sixth grade:

To Eric Lindstrom, a beautiful streem [sic]

How I long to know you
to see within your soul
your [sic] like a mountin [sic] streem [sic]
Oh that I could wade in that streem [sic]
My fascination with you draws me so near
And I am afraid that I will fall in
Oh lovely streem [sic], happy streem [sic]
I am . . .

The poem mercifully ends there, although it's clear that the last line should read:

I am . . .
luv [sic], luv [sic], luv [sic].

Sex messes up everything. I'm obsessed by sex because I am American and all Americans are obsessed by sex. The rest of the world thinks we're crazy. The rest of the world can't believe that sex impeached our president. Then again, our nation's capital is a town that lives in the shadow of the world's largest dick, the Washington Monument. I believe that giant, looming five-hundred-foot phallus has warped everyone's thinking in this country. I remain convinced that there will never be a woman president until somebody digs a five-hundred-foot tunnel honoring Eleanor Roosevelt.

Our obsession with sex has made America the porn capital of the world. It isn't much of a stretch to say that porn may be fueling the boom of the new Internet economy. I'm not against porn, but I will confess that, personally, I just don't get it. I am extremely self-centered, and I don't like things that don't involve me directly. For example, I can't even watch the food channel because all I can think is "Where's my baked Alaska?" If I watch porn, all I can think is "Where's my really ugly guy from New Jersey with a hairy back and a bizarrely large penis?"

I recently went into my local video store, and on the return shelf I saw a movie, *Gang Bang Twelve*. I asked the pierced and tattooed surfer boy behind the counter, "Are there really twelve of these?"

"Get real," he replied. "They're on like sixteen or seventeen now."

I started wondering, who were the fans of the *Gang Bang* oeuvre? If you were watching *Gang Bang Twelve* and you had not seen *Gang Bang Eleven*, would you be hopelessly confused? Would the intricate plotting and subtle character arcs be completely lost to those who hadn't invested the time to watch the entire *Gang Bang* decaseptology?

Are the *Gang Bang*–ophiles incredibly picky about minute details of casting and performance? Do they sit around at the inevitable *Gang Bang* conventions and get into arcane discussions about *Bang Seven* vs. *Bang Eight*?

"That Meryl Strip can't act to save her life."

"I agree, she's a dreadful actress, even worse than Joan

Cusuck. Why, I didn't believe for a moment that she was being gang-banged at all. And the wardrobe was wretched, and don't get me started on the special effects."

Or do they just jack off in their living rooms? I'm not judging, of course. I am as obsessed by sex as anyone, maybe—no surely—more. I just don't see sex as a spectator sport, any more than eating or lying in the sun or getting a massage. Frankly I don't even see most spectator sports as spectator sports. I love to kick around a soccer ball but would go into a coma if forced to watch other people do it. I love to do things that feel good, but I have no intention of wasting my time watching somebody else get to do them.

I, like most people, have had my own horrifying, inexplicable sex fantasies that shock even me. When Howard Stern—yes, that Howard Stern—came to my house in L.A. for my friend Mary's birthday party, he proved to be charming and polite, and he didn't say a word about my rack, or anyone else's.

I then proceeded to have a series of embarrassingly torrid sexual dreams involving Howard Stern, a man who has made millions bragging about his small, poorly functioning love piston. I could have anyone in my dreams, so why Howard Stern? What was I thinking? On the other hand, my question is this: How small could his throbbing man-pole be? I mean, the guy is a hundred feet tall. My personal opinion, based on no empirical facts whatsoever, is that he's reverse bragging, to get sympathy. As to the alleged poor taste of my subconscious, I have no good defense. True to my program, I must embrace all of my sexuality, even my cheap, tawdry Howard Stern sex dreams.

When my sex life has caused me more problems than I care to name, I have often reverted to the fantasy that I might be a lesbian. It would be so interesting and exotic. After all, noted anthropologist Margaret Mead once said, "I think extreme heterosexuality is a perversion." Besides, it would be so interesting and exotic to be a lesbian. I loved the whole idea of it and felt it would solve a lot of problems. The fact that I had never been sexually attracted to women was a minor detail I'd just sort of refuse to think about, the way Scarlett O'Hara refused to think about the Civil War. In fact, when I forced myself to consider the sex part, I had the same reaction I used to have when my brother tried to tell me something I didn't feel like hearing: I did the mental equivalent of sticking my fingers in my ears and singing the national anthem really loud.

So me and this girl are naked, in bed—

"Oh, say can you see! By the dawn's early light!"

I'm serious, we're naked, and we're kissing, and then she reaches down and—

"What so proudly we hailed from the twilight's last gleaming."

It would go on like that until I finally gave up. All I can say is that if I ever do go to bed with a woman, I sure hope she's patriotic.

I became obsessed with the idea that I *ought* to be a lesbian when I had a celebrity sighting of the most famous lesbian couple going, Ellen DeGeneres and Anne Heche. This was of course prior to their much-publicized breakup, which saddened me greatly.

They were adorably kind to one another as they were shopping in one of my favorite little boutiques. Ellen was looking at this gorgeous and ridiculously expensive coat. She was saying that she loved it, but that it was too expensive, especially what with the new house and everything. Anne snatched it up, pardon the verb choice, and said that she insisted on buying it for Ellen, because it would look beautiful on Ellen, and Ellen deserved it, and if Ellen didn't have it, she'd always wish that she had just gone and bought it.

At that moment, I became seized with jealousy. Oh, sure, I could find a man who would buy me some cute coat, but he would never understand, would never really know, deep in the core of his being, why I *needed* it. I would never have that kind of shopping intimacy with a man, ever. Frankly, that seemed worth giving some girl head.

The potentially sad truth is I like men. I like their bodies, their big, knuckley hands, hairy legs, and broad, sweaty shoulders. Yes, I am aware that some marvelous dykes have all that and more.

But they don't have throbbing love trumpets. No, they don't have rigid shafts of tumescent longing, or pounding engorged manhoods, or pulsing rods of desire, or stiff aching lust scepters, or pumping passion poles or languorous love javelins, or jolting joysticks, or plain old big hard cocks.

Or rather, they do, but they are battery-operated, and it's just not the same. For me.

So I am forced to embrace my white-bread, straight-up, dull Midwestern heterosexuality, and all of its tedious and predictable consequences.

Pregnancy is of course one of the more exciting heterosexual consequences, and yet I have always sought to avoid it, sure that motherhood would be something at which I would fail miserably. I worried about getting pregnant from the day I realized that I could. Even before I had intercourse, I was sure that there would be some weird pregnancy loophole that I would fall through. Those of us raised in Christianity are already primed for the idea of beating the odds when it comes to conception. I remember seriously worrying that if some guy jacked off in one of Minnesota's ten thousand lakes, and the water was really warm, and I went for a swim, I might get pregnant. I'd seen some pretty shady-looking guys by Turtle Lake, which was very warm by August. I actually called Planned Parenthood in Minneapolis, to pose this Turtle Lake conception scenario, and they said it was unlikely.

Not impossible though, just unlikely.

Though I am completely in awe of the miracle of birth, I am completely repulsed by the concept of baby showers. If I ever take my Grrl Genius platform to the White House, I will begin by signing a decree banning baby showers.

That sounds harsh and cruel, I know, but I have my reasons. I'm not against the giving of presents, or the gathering of friends, I'm against traditional baby showers.

I went to my friend Sandra's baby shower recently. Let me say that she is a national treasure, her husband is a living doll, and that they have chosen to reproduce restores my faith in the future of the human race.

Having said that, I confess that I was miserable at her baby shower. I arrived, and a friend, who was apparently cheesed off that I hadn't given her up-to-the-minute reports on my marital distress, attacked me like a starved rottweiler as I made my way to the buffet table.

"So what's going on?" she demanded. "I heard you guys are back together."

I whispered, hoping for once not to attract attention, "Actually, we're not, at the moment. It's a really difficult time."

I assumed that would put a halt to the inquisition, but apparently she was just getting started. She began rapidly firing off questions loudly as though she were a reporter attending a press conference on my personal dysfunction.

"Well, what are you doing? I mean, are you going to get a divorce or aren't you? I heard he won't go to counseling anymore...."

I was really too stunned to respond, which was a good thing. I simply sat there, feeling like an island of domestic failure in a sea of domestic tranquillity.

Then it was time for the "party game." It started off simple, and sweet: we were each to guess the day and time of Sandra's delivery. Whoever won the pool would get a lovely prize. This would be a potentially charming little amusement if left alone. Since there was apparently a control-freak convention in town, it couldn't just be left at that.

One of the women piped up, "Oh, and be sure to tell us all your name, and how you know Sandra."

Okay, our name, and how we know Sandra, and the date and the time of the baby's birth. That's doable, I thought.

Then a bossy Englishwoman from the corner of the room chimed in, "I would so love it if you would each tell us what your profession is."

My inner Lurch started grumbling. I don't like talking about work, and I consider "And what do you do?" to be one of the most boorish and rude party questions imaginable. It's rude because I am often unemployed.

The Englishwoman couldn't let it go at that: "And tell us your romantic status, so we can get to *know* you better!"

My grumbling was now at a dull roar. Naturally, I had to go first.

"I'm Cathryn Michon, I know Sandra through a mutual friend, I'm a comic and a writer and an actress, and a singer. I think the baby will be born September tenth, because that's when the manuscript of my book is due, and my marriage is in shambles."

A roomful of women in flowered sundresses gaped at me in dumb horror. Then, they burst out laughing, because they mistakenly assumed I was kidding. Everyone who went after me wisely left off the romantic-status part, and pretty soon, they stopped telling about their careers as well. Naturally, when it was the pushy English broad's turn, she didn't say spit about anything personal, nothing about her job or her "romantic life."

"What's your job?" I barked out belligerently from my

sarcasm isolation booth. "You're the one that made us tell our jobs, so what's your job?"

"Oh," she demurred, "I'm a designer."

"A designer of what?" I wanted to shout out. "How much money do you make? Did you have an orgasm the last time you had sex with your husband? Whatever made you think that was a good outfit to wear to this party? I just want to get to *know* you better!"

Of course I said none of those things. Then it was time for the interminable opening of the presents, an exercise that would allow us to explore the space-time continuum in exciting new ways, to see if, as Einstein (and probably his wife) postulated, time is in fact elastic and can stretch to ridiculous proportions where minutes become millennia.

The seemingly endless gift-opening is actually most horrifying for the receiver, who is forced to exclaim breathlessly about rather dull merchandise over and over and over again.

"Oh my God, this is the most adorable receiving blanket!"

Yes, isn't it, not like the other seven horrifying receiving blankets she had to extol the virtues of just a few epochs ago, before the glaciers moved through and created the Rocky Mountains. Yes, the Eeyores that cover this receiving blanket are vastly superior to the duckies and teddy bears and big-crying-eye girls we've seen so far. Thank God this baby can now be wrapped in a blanket covered in the image of a terminally depressed donkey. Whatever happens, don't receive your baby in any receiving blanket that isn't covered in Eeyores, no other licensed character will do, God only knows what will happen if you do, because *this Eeyore blanket is the most adorable receiving blanket ever devised by humankind!*

Then the poor mother-to-be is further tortured by having to say again and again how "small" and how "tiny" each garment is. Isn't it amazing how small the socks are, how tiny the shoes are? Yes, they are small, they are tiny, because, in fact, babies are *very small people.* Hence the smallness and the tininess of the garments. This is not a revelation nor is it clever on the part of the gift givers to have purchased such incredibly minute versions of hats and sweaters and vests. In fact, it would have been wildly inappropriate if someone had shown up with size XXL coveralls from the Big and Tall Men's Shop because babies are *very small and tiny people who wear very small and tiny clothes!*

After the presents are opened and everyone, except the person who needs it most, is fully in the bag from the champagne punch, all the grizzled birth vets start telling the mom-to-be their bitter war stories. Honestly, what could be more comforting to someone about to face a potentially fatal physical endeavor than to hear things like:

"When they cut me for my episiotomy, I swear he slit me practically up to my naval. It was like a wind tunnel in there for almost six months."

"I had what they call a delinquent uterus, and when I was pushing out the placenta, my whole uterus came flying out and just plopped onto the floor like a dead fish."

"I'm telling you, I was in such agony, and I was so determined not to have drugs, so I just asked my husband to shoot me. And he did. And it was *that* gunshot wound that helped me to ride it out without the epidural."

Okay, nobody got shot, but the point is, the other two stories are real. Stories that were told at a lovely catered event with nice floral arrangements.

Some people defend this kind of behavior, they say that traditional baby showers are a ritual. That's no kind of reason at all. Aztec sacrifices were a ritual too, but eventually someone realized that they were, you know, a really bad idea!

My friend Marlene suggested that I was overly hostile to

this particular baby shower because my marriage is, in fact, in a shambles, and I'm sure that I will never have children of my own. I told her to fuck off. Which I always do when she is right.

Marlene is separated from her husband too. We decided that if we each end up alone, we will go in together on adopting one of those precious Chinese baby girls who has been abandoned. Since I'm insecure about my potential as a mother, I like that this situation has a low bar for success. I might not be the best mother, but at least I didn't leave her under a tree to dehydrate, so by default I'm better than the mother she had. We keep calling our imaginary baby Suzy Wong, because I love those little dresses she always wore. I still don't know if I'm capable of taking care of a baby, but at least little Suzy Wong seems like a viable option if I ever get more confident about it.

I would still ban traditional baby showers if I were the president. I would legislate that henceforth baby showers would consist of everyone getting spa treatments, lovely facials and manicures and massages, and the presents would be left by the door for the mom-to-be to open quietly, by herself, remembering to keep the gift tags for the six defective receiving blankets that aren't covered in depressed donkeys.

I'd like to say that, as a result of vigorously working my Grrl Genius program, today my Grrl Genius sexuality, which I celebrate and cherish, no longer rules my life or makes me act like an enormous idiot.

That, however, would be a big fat lie.

I am always confusing sex with love, and I'm not even sure I know what love is, further confusing the matter. Turning back to my childhood diaries, I find that my definitions of love have always been sketchy at best. In third grade I was asked to write on the topic of love. It was for Valentine's Day, a day many people associate with love, but one I somehow always associate with the massacre. The assignment was "Tell us what you think love is."

Love Is

My cat always sleeps with me. She is very kind to me. For some examples, she does what I say and pushes her nose agenst [sic] my moth [sic].

My definition of love being someone who will sleep with me and push their nose agenst my moth has held fast in all the love relationships that were to follow. Doing what I say, sadly, never has been a trend amongst my loved ones.

Recently, I concluded that my husband and I had reached an impasse in therapy. I decided to tell my husband that I would be filing for divorce. It was one of the worst days of my life. It was as if I had decided to attend a Puppy Murdering Festival, and I was the head puppy murderer. One of my duties as head puppy murderer was to tell my husband I wanted a divorce, and so I did. We both cried, and it was awful, but I felt it was the right decision.

Then, a few days later, we were having sex. A lot.

The good thing about it was that it was great sex. I mean, it's been many, many years since sex has felt so wrong, so *bad*. That is, of course, an enormous turn-on. Just ask the thousands of dentists and attorneys and car salesmen who are, even at this moment, strapped in leather harnesses in suburban dungeons all over America, being told that they are very, very naughty boys, and that they will be punished, oh yes, they will be punished.

The bad thing about this postbreakup sex is that it is so wrong, so *bad,* and I have a sneaking feeling that I will be punished, oh yes, I will be punished.

So now our divorce is on hold. We are talking about trying to work things out. He's not a bad person, I'm not a bad person, maybe we can solve all our problems, it's certainly worth a try.

Where I go to take yoga, there are a lot of free New Agey magazines by the door. The kind of magazines that have ads for places where you can get your chakras cleansed or your aura rotated, or where to find a reputable pet psychic, if, in fact, there is such a thing. Though I go to psychics all the time, I'm wary of pet psychics because there's no accountability. Your dog can never say:

"That is so not true! I don't eat the cat poops because I feel abandoned when my people go to work, I eat them because they are delectable, covered as they are in a light, crunchy coating of cat litter. They're like doggy Almond Roca, and I cannot get enough of them!"

Anyway there is a new magazine in the pile at the yoga center called *Divorce Magazine.* Apparently *Festering Emotional Wound Monthly* was too long and *Failure Digest* just wasn't sexy enough. Anyway, *Divorce Magazine,* which seems to be mostly filled with ads for lawyers and waterproof mascara, says that this postbreakup sex is not that uncommon, and they seem to think it's not that great an idea. It also says that it's not a reason to stay together and may be masking the real, underlying issues that cannot be resolved.

Whatever.

I don't know what to think. All I know is that my husband is still, to me, the most heartachingly attractive man at any party. Over the years together, you memorize the other person's body in a way that is almost impossible to let go of. I have detailed information stored in my brain about things like all the little brown-sugar-colored freckles on his shoulder, and all the patterns they can make while I'm waiting for him to wake up on a Sunday morning. The one that looks like a cat, the one that looks like a duck. How do you forget about the pattern of the freckles? Do you stay together for the freckles?

I'm obsessed about all this sex we're having, and deep, hard questions keep thrusting into my mind.

Should a Grrl Genius stay married for the sex?

Should a Grrl Genius get divorced except for the sex?

Is any of this really about sex at all?

For the answers to these dilemmas I turn back to my childhood diaries, skipping forward to high school. Unfortunately I find good advice. From my mother, of all people.

IMPORTANT QUESTIONS MOM SAYS TO ASK ABOUT POTENTIAL BOYFRIENDS:

1. Does this person care how you feel, what you do or accomplish?

2. Would he make a neat possession? Do you think of him that way?

3. Does he run down your vision of yourself?

4. Can he accept you as you are? Can you accept him as he is?

5. Does he already know where he wants to go and would you tend to get in the way?

6. Does he care for you the way you care for him or is it a one-sided martyrdom?

Those are tough, good questions, and, of course, there is nothing there about sex or freckles. My mother hasn't said a thing about my separation, except to say that she would support me no matter what happens.

Although, come to think of it, she did send the frigging diaries. She sent me written records of everything I wanted to become as a grown-up. I get to decide if I have become that person or not.

My mother is the original Grrl Genius. She won't talk about sex, but apparently she knows a little something about it.

How very annoying.

A GRRL GENIUS FACTOID

Men are twice as likely to get acne as Grrl Geniuses.

A GRRL GENIUS LITTLE PINK POST-IT

Hey, Grrl Genius!

Did you know that your fat makes you sexy? Your sex hormones need body fat to survive and thrive. To be model-thin, which requires being 23 percent leaner than the average woman, usually means that you will have problems with infertility and hormone imbalance, which can lead to ovarian cancer, endometriosis, and osteoporosis.

Mmmm, hollow bones, that's sexy.

Of course it's actually not sexy at all. It's been clinically proven that women with normal or above normal body fat are way better in bed. As Naomi Wolf points out in her classic work of Grrl Genius, *The Beauty Myth,* "Studies consistently show that with dietary deprivation, sexual interests dissipate. Subjects of one experiment stopped masturbating or having sexual fantasies at 1,700 calories a day." Another study found that on scales of erotic excitability and readiness, plumper Grrls outscored skinny Grrls two to one.

If you want to be sexy, really sexy, and by that I mean capable of actually *having sex,* eat a goddamned sandwich, Grrl Genius!

Step Eight

"Sought to Reject Penis Envy"

War is birth envy.

—Anonymous

I wonder why men can get serious at all.
They have this delicate long thing hanging
outside their bodies, which goes up and down
by its own will. . . . If I were a man, I would
always be laughing at myself.

—Yoko Ono

I will tell you flat out right now that Grrl Geniuses do not have penis envy. I like penises just fine, they are very handy, but I don't care to have one attached to me, thank you very much. Just as I don't care to have an electric can opener attached to me. When I need one, I'll get one. Just because a thing is handy doesn't mean I need it to be attached to me, I am not a Swiss Army Grrl. So here in step eight of the "Journey to Genius" we must reject penis envy. We must debunk it for what it is, Freud's own wet dream. It's quite adorable that Sigmund thought we wanted a willy of our own, but of course we do not.

Penis envy is completely ridiculous; on the other hand, penis worship can be a lovely hobby for a Grrl Genius, as long as it doesn't cut into our other important Grrl Genius activities. Don't let it make you late for the Barneys clearance sale.

What I want to know is how come no one ever talked about womb envy? When my sister-in-law Maria had a baby, I was invited to attend. It's the most amazing thing I've ever seen. Sure, I had seen people giving birth in documentary movies and such, but I am here to tell you that the difference between seeing live birth in a movie and seeing it in real life is like the difference between watching *E.T.* and actually being abducted and anally probed by aliens.

The astounding thing about the birth of my niece is that it was a *two-day labor. Two-day labor!* And it was really hard . . . on me. There were many reasons for this. My shoes were uncomfortable, and I didn't sleep much, and I had some bad take-out food.

I have never given birth. Now I'm starting to wonder if I ever will. Looking back on my lifelong quest to avoid pregnancy, I have to say that birth control is one of those things I just cannot get enough of. The pill is just an appetizer for me. Condoms, diaphragms, foam, whatever.

Honestly, if I could build a dam of mud and twigs up there, I would.

My zeal for birth control hasn't prevented me from panicking about being pregnant, usually about once a month. That's how I got hooked on the early pregnancy test, or E.P.T. Now, the E.P.T. is a pretty hard test—I mean, it's not the SAT, but still. It's hard, because it involves peeing on sticks, which is not something I am good at. Once you see that blue line and know that you aren't pregnant, it's the best high ever. Those tests only cost five or six bucks, and you can fly on that adrenaline buzz all morning. In fact, I wish there were other early-warning tests, like an Early Failure Test, or an Early Fatness Test. I'd like to get up first thing in the morning, pee on all my sticks, know for sure that I'm not a failure, I'm not fat, and I'm not pregnant, so let's take on the day!

Even though I am currently in no position to have a baby, that did nothing to mitigate the awe I felt attending Maria's previously mentioned, and I really can't emphasize this enough, **TWO-DAY LABOR.**

About a day and a half into the **AGONIZING TWO THOUSAND EIGHT HUNDRED AND EIGHTY MINUTES OF LABOR, WHICH YOU CAN ALSO THINK OF AS EQUIVA-LENT TO SIXTY-FOUR CONSECUTIVE SCRAPEY, SCRAPEY DENTAL-PLAQUE CLEANINGS' WORTH OF LABOR,** Maria's OB came in and told her that Maria should try some "nipple stim," which is apparently a technical term for "mess around with your tits a little." Supposedly the sexual stimulation kick-starts your uterus into high gear.

A little while later I came back into the room with some bad take-out food, and there was my baby brother, Teddy, doing the Lord's work with the nipple stim. He was morti-fied to see me, and I was embarrassed, and he said, "Oh, I'm sorry, you really shouldn't have to see this."

I replied, "You know what, at this point I would blow her myself if it would make the baby come out faster."

So I guess we set a new boundary there.

This baby, a little girl, was to be named after me, and I'll never forget when Teddy and Maria called to tell me this.

"So we've been kickin' it around about the baby's name, and we've decided on Maya Cathryn Michon."

I instantly became a giant blob of gooey, embarrassing emotions, completely unable to speak. Finally I said, "Um, does the, um, Cathryn part have anything to do with the fact that, you know, my name is Cathryn?"

One of my brother's customary long silences ensued, and then he yelled to his wife in the other room, "Hey, Maria, guess what, her name is Cathryn too, so it works out perfect!"

When Miss Maya Cathryn Michon (Grrl Genius) finally arrived after ONE HUNDRED AND SEVENTY-TWO THOUSAND AND EIGHT HUNDRED SECONDS OF LABOR, WHICH YOU CAN ALSO THINK OF AS NINETY-SIX EPISODES OF A HORRIFYINGLY UNFUNNY SITCOM LIKE *SHE'S THE SHERIFF* WORTH OF LABOR, she came out into the world with her perfect little hand curled into a perfect little fist, and her chin resting on that hand. She looked exactly like one of those really cheesy Kmart studio portraits, but it wasn't cheesy at all because she was stunning. Of course, she is a genius and beautiful and talented, and it was a miracle, and there is no other way to put it.

The next day I had to go home, probably for some stupid job thing that seemed important at the time. My brother and I were racing to the airport with seconds to spare, as is our family custom, and I made it onto the flight one minute before the door shut, and as I plunked down into my seat, I burst into tears. Not those sniffly, cute, girl-in-a-Lifetime-movie-of-the-week tears, no these would be the big, drooly, hiccuppy, racking sobs. I cry plenty, but not like this, and I wasn't handling it well. So I decided to make my way to the bathroom, and the stewardess did her best to block me, making good use of her considerable hairdo, but I blew past her, telling her that I was about to be sick.

So there I was, in the bathroom, trying desperately to get my sorry act together, when I hear the pilot come over the loudspeaker: "We can't push away from the gate because there's someone in the bathroom."

Yes, my favorite nightmare had finally come true: an entire planeload of people were officially hating me for being in the bathroom. I slowly opened the door and saw *two hundred and forty-seven* people giving me the evil eye, because I was the one thing that stood between them and a little slice of heaven called Burbank, California.

I slithered back up the aisle and back into my seat, avoiding the hundreds of angry stares. The Qiana-wearing slacker next to me poked me on the shoulder and said, "We totally knew it was you in the bathroom!" Well, thank you, Captain Obvious, I thought.

I rode home to Burbank, reveling in my newfound "potty fame" and wondering what exactly it was that had made me fall apart, what had made me so emotional? I knew what it was of course, it was this brand-new person. A brand-new person whom I had just met, and I already missed her so much that it was like a dull, throbbing ache.

At that moment, I realized that penis envy wasn't just misguided, it was downright delusional. It should obviously be womb envy, or nothing. I once had an old boyfriend who was proud that he could open the bathroom door with his penis. Dubious achievement? Sure. But he was proud of it. Fine. But here's the deal: I can make a spleen, right out of my own body, and I don't even know what a spleen does, or where it goes. I can make brains and eyeballs out of Twinkies and Snapple! That's pure Grrl Genius! And, if I'm willing to put in **EIGHT THOUSAND SIX HUNDRED AND FORTY-SEVEN CONSECUTIVE BIKINI WAXES' WORTH OF LABOR,** I can give birth to that baby. My sister-in-law Maria is a Grrl Genius, all moms are Grrl Geniuses, and when a guy can pull off that kind of everyday miracle, I'll be jealous of his wanker. In the meantime, I'll use my hand to open the bathroom door, thank you very much.

A GRRL GENIUS LITTLE PINK POST-IT

Hey, Grrl Genius!

Even though Bill Gates has all the money on earth, it's a little-known fact that a Grrl Genius was actually the first computer programmer. Lady Augusta Ada Byron Love-lace devised a punch-card program that would tell an "analytic engine," or computer, exactly what to do. Plus, what about how cool her name is?

Another woman, Grace Hopper, a naval officer, was responsible for inventing the first computer "compiler" in the 1950s. It streamlined computer programming and was the beginning of the "user-friendly" revolution. She didn't get a dime extra for her brilliant invention, but you can be sure that as a navy rear admiral she has gotten plenty of hilarious jokes about her ass.

Joni Mitchell

A GRRL GENIUS PROFILE IN EXCELLENCE

(Also a shameless way of sucking up to a celebrity
I would give anything to meet)

Joni Mitchell is one of the greatest artists in rock history;
not one of the greatest women, one of the greatest
period. That she was belatedly inducted into the Rock
and Roll Hall of Fame is a disgrace. That she doesn't
simply have her own Hall of Fame devoted entirely to
celebrating her Grrl Genius 365 days a year is an even
bigger disgrace.

She is an amazing singer, and one of the greatest
songwriters of her generation, as she effortlessly moves
back and forth between the worlds of rock, folk, and jazz.
Both her music and lyrics are masterful, and she is also a
world-class painter.

You might also notice that she looks a lot like me.

Joni Mitchell fans are more than familiar with the fact
that she had a daughter, the infamous "little green,"
whom she gave up for adoption.

I believe that I am "little green." This is not an indict-
ment of my (obviously) adoptive mother, whom I totally
consider to be my "real mother." But I can no longer
pretend that I am not the daughter of Don Juan's
Reckless Daughter.

I understand, from *People* magazine, that a girl has
come forward who claims to be Joni's daughter, but let's
look at the cold facts. This "daughter" does not sing at
all, whereas I, like Joni, am a three-octave soprano. This
"daughter" looks nothing like Joni, whereas I cannot set
foot in a room where there are musicians without someone going on and on about how much I look like Joni.

I don't need to have Joni acknowledge me as her
daughter, I don't even want that. I have no desire to
drive a wedge between Joni and this alleged "daughter"
who mistakenly believes that she and Joni are genetically
linked. Love knows nothing of the boundaries of genetics, and that's how it should be.

All I want is to play Joni in the miniseries of her Grrl
Genius life that so desperately needs to be made. Why is
this miniseries not in preproduction even as we speak?
All I want is to help the world celebrate the genius of
Joni.

Joni Mitchell, I love you, and your Grrl Genius!

Step Nine

"Came to Believe in a Grrrl Genius Higher Power Greater Than Ourselves"

Lead me not into temptation,
I can find the way myself.

—RITA MAE BROWN

When we talk to God, we're praying,
when God talks to us, we're schizophrenic.

—JANE WAGNER

You don't have to be dowdy to be a Christian.

—TAMMY FAE BAKKER

The Grrl Genius Guide to Life, like any good twelve-step program, involves the use of a higher power. You can choose to have your higher power be something as arbitrary as poorly dressed fashion tyrant Mr. Blackwell, or it could be the miraculous healing power of chocolate, or a really excellent brand of high-quality face cream, (I personally recommend Guerlain Issima Aquaserum, expensive and worth every penny).

Or, you could chose as your higher power the traditional omnipotent loving goddess, creatrix of all things seen and unseen, or your higher power could be a mean, old, crabby white guy who sends plagues and locusts. The point of the program is this: it's entirely up to you. If you choose to make the great leap forward to Grrl Geniushood, you're going to have to start making some high-level genius decisions, including choosing whom you want to be the omnipotent power that rules the universe, the creator, or creatrix, of all things seen and unseen. That's part of the price of your genius.

When I try to envision my higher power, I usually imagine Maya Angelou, because I so enjoy her work on Oprah's book club. She has the most magisterial speaking voice, and I understand that she's quite the talented poet and novelist as well. If I'm thinking of a guy, I'm usually thinking James Earl Jones. Not the scary Darth Vader James Earl Jones, but the deeply confident "Verizon" James Earl Jones. Clearly, I have had enough of the idea of God being an old white guy, as I never imagine God as that creepy Ensure grandpa who's always promising to marry his little granddaughter, as he happily chugs his vitamin-fortified beverage so that he can "keep up with her."

I was raised Episcopalian, which was exotic in Minnesota, where everyone was either Catholic or Lutheran. My religious affiliation got even more exciting when I discovered in grade school that since my mother's parents were self-loathing lapsed Jews, I was technically a Jew. No one in Minnesota was Jewish.

I latched onto the Jewish thing instantly: if something didn't work out for me, it was obviously due to the rampant anti-Semitism that had plagued me and my people back since, well, the plagues. If I didn't get picked for a team by Paul Amerongen, the sweetest, kindest boy on our block and also the neighborhood athletic coordinator for softball, I would assume a tragic, haunted attitude and say, "It's because I'm Jewish, isn't it?"

Paul responded honestly by saying, "What are you talking about? I don't even know what that is."

I would reply wearily, "*Oy gevalt,* don't get me started." I never bothered to learn anything about Judaism, I just randomly used phrases I picked up from *Fiddler on the Roof,* which I had seen at the Chanhassen Dinner Theater. For an entire summer I wandered around the house answering simple questions by saying things like "Right? Of course, right," and muttering about the need for more "Tradition!"

Even though I was raised Christian, I was always bothered by the relentlessly male focus of the whole Father, Son, and Holy Ghost monopoly. The situation got worse for me with Dana, the seminary student who molested me at age fourteen. After feeling me up and sticking his tongue down my throat, he informed me that all my Jewish relatives were going to hell because they weren't "saved." Apparently to him, being "saved" meant you could chase all the prepubescent tail you wanted, which was a new twist on the old "What would Jesus do?" question Dana was so fond of posing.

My problems with the non-Grrl-Genius-friendly nature of the Christian Church began early. From the time she was a small child, my friend Denise Steiner wanted to be a Catholic priest. Her mother, Laurie, was very liberal and never wanted to discourage her children from pursuing their heart's desires, however ludicrous they may have been.

Mrs. Steiner was so accommodating that when her youngest daughter, Jeanne Marie, insisted at age five that she was a boy and her name was now Bob, we were all instructed to "just go along with it" and to agree that she was now a boy, a boy named Bob. We went on that way for years, calling Jeanne Marie "Bob," until around the time she started to get pointy little breast buds, and even then it was up to her to call off the whole "Bob" situation.

As far as Denise's desire to be a priest, Mrs. Steiner was all for it. She had a sister who was a nun, and we could all see that it was a crap job with terrible outfits. So Mrs. Steiner told Denise to write to the pope and tell him she wanted to be a priest and to ask him to kindly explain why she couldn't.

Every year Denise would write the pope, and every year she would get back a letter on heavy, embossed Vatican stationery, explaining why she couldn't be a priest. Apparently, the letters would be updated every year, because they were always different. This led us to believe that we were making progress with the pope and that he was actually taking the time to consider our arguments.

We would lie around in the backyard, eating vanilla-orange ice cream push-ups and trying to think of new ways to trip up the pope and get him to see our point of view. I was sure it was only a matter of time before the pontiff would come around.

"Okay. Let's get serious about this thing," I'd say, licking a random drop of ice cream wedged between my fingers. "What did he say in that 'God became flesh' part?"

Denise would read from the letter, now sticky from the push-ups, one of the all-time most inefficient ice cream delivery systems, "Blah blah blah . . . oh, here it is. 'We can only assume that because when God became of the flesh, through our risen Lord Jesus Christ, he chose to be a man. Because of this, we understand that it is God's will that men should head his church here on earth.'"

Denise angrily shoved the pope's letter back in her pocket. "Just because Jesus happened to be a guy. That is just so butt stupid."

I wasn't willing to give up, though. I knew there had to be a way around this ridiculously lame argument.

"Wait a minute, what about this?" I said. "Why don't we ask the pope what it would mean if Jesus had been twins, like, you know, the kind of twins where one is a boy and one is a girl, like Marsha and Mark Enfield who live over on Holton? What if it had been like, Jesus and Debbie Christ?"

"Oh, please, that sucks. The pope will just say that Jesus would have been the one who was born first, and so Jesus would still be the son of God and Debbie would be first runner-up, or whatever."

Denise, who was notoriously limber, hung one-legged from the monkey bars but still managed to keep her ice cream perfectly parallel to the ground.

"Okay, okay, okay, what about this?" I said, "What if Jesus and Debbie Christ were Siamese twins, like Chang and Eng, and they both came out of their mom at the exact same time?"

Denise sucked hard on her push-up. "That stinks too. The pope is just going to say that God wouldn't have let Jesus be any kind of twins at all, God would be in charge of it, God for sure wouldn't let Jesus be some stupid birth defect."

"Okay, fine. . . . But still, if God can prevent birth defects, then why are there birth defects?"

It was a good question, if somewhat off the topic.

"Look," Denise said, "you just have to accept that he's going to win this thing."

This is exactly what I refused to accept. As far as I was concerned, we had the pope on the ropes. "That's not true, if we can make a really good argument, he could come around."

"Don't you get it? The pope is always going to win because the pope gets to make all the stinking rules."

Of course Denise turned out to be right. When she grew up, she didn't become a priest, or a nun either, she became a kindergarten teacher, so now at least she gets to make all the stinking rules. Years later, Mrs. Steiner's sister Cindy, "Sister Cindy,"ended up falling in love with a foxy priest. They both quit their Church jobs so they could get married, have sex, and wear decent-looking clothes.

I still wonder what would have happened if Jesus and Debbie Christ, as the conjoined twin Prince and Princess of Peace, had founded the Christian Church. I wonder if so many unscrupulous people would have bothered to hijack Christianity. Probably not.

It seems every time I turn on the television there is some pockmarked man, in a suit so ugly that no one will think he has the flair for fashion that is the certain mark of homosexuality, pontificating in his native "Booger Holler" dialect about the fact that the Bible specifically forbids homosexuality and abortion. No one is ever on the TV to point out that Jesus never said spit about either homosexuality or abortion, even though both were common practices in his day.

The angry white man never seems to mention that the Bible also says that it's A-okay to keep slaves and sacrifice your firstborn son, but an abomination to have a mortgage or a credit card. These troublesome "facts" never seem to affect the man in the wretched suit's opinions about God's absolute word as expressed through the Bible, a document that has had more bad rewrites than an overbudget Kevin Costner movie.

My favorite part of these right-wing Christian TV appearances is when the Bible-thumper or his smug wife, with her impossibly gravity-defying shelf of mall hair, starts in about Sodom and Gomorrah. They always seem to feel that this Sodom and Gomorrah story is the key to God's alleged hatred of gay people.

What's odd is, if you actually go and read that story in the Bible, you'll be shocked about how it seems to have nothing to do with gay people at all. In my Grrl Genius estimation, it's a fully lame and pointless story jam-packed with so much trashy heterosexual behavior that it makes your typical episode of *Jerry Springer* look like *Masterpiece Theatre*.

In the story of Sodom and Gomorrah, God, who for some reason has no idea what is going on down in the world, has to send an undercover angel to visit this guy Lot over in Sodom, so that God can see "Whassup!" with earth. Astute TV viewers will recognize this as the premise of the fantastic Michael Landon TV series *Highway to Heaven*.

Not too long after the angel shows up, a bunch of Lot's toothless neighbors get all liquored up and decide they don't like this new "angel feller." They head over to Lot's place to gang-rape the angel, as their clever little way of saying "get outta Dodge." But Lot, who takes this hosting thing way too seriously, convinces the local yokels not to rape his houseguest, because that would be very impolite. Instead, Lot suggests that the yokels help themselves to Lot's two virgin daughters. So the girls are happily packed off to the gang bang, and the angel, whom Lot doesn't even really know, is spared all the messy inconvenience of being raped.

God then decides to blow up the town of Sodom, but

not because it's gay. Sodom wasn't exactly San Francisco, with lots of cute art boutiques and excellent drag shows. It wasn't the gayness of the place that cheesed God off. God messes up Sodom because it was loaded with equal-opportunity rapists who were more than happy to swing both ways depending on who was being offered up as the victim du jour. God doesn't bust Sodom's chops for being "Gayland," he torches the place for being "Rapeland."

It's very unclear to me just what exactly Gomorrah's problem was, except that it was basically too close to Sodom. Evidently, even when it comes to God's infernal wrath, it's important to remember the mantra "location, location, location."

Still, the story seems pointless in terms of God punishing the wicked, because "Pimp Daddy" Lot, who is obviously the worst father ever, escapes from Sodom completely scot-free. Lot just heads off to the hills with his daughters, where, in a move too nasty even for the *Springer* show, he knocks up both of his girls. The only person in Lot's family who gets punished is Lot's wife, who gets turned into a human salt lick, apparently just for being so uppity as to look in the rearview mirror.

From my Grrl Genius point of view, it seems to me that with the cavalier way God takes out Lot's wife, if God was against anybody in this story, he was against women. Certainly if this story is the Bible's best shot at proving that God hates gay people, it could not be a more poorly constructed argument. Besides, if God really was that worked up about gay people, it surely wouldn't have been too much trouble to add an eleventh commandment, something along the lines of "I almost forgot, thou really shouldn't be gay."

Certainly Jesus could have mentioned the whole gay situation. A terrific place would have been in that story about not stoning the woman who committed adultery. Jesus could have said something like "Let whoever among you who has not sinned cast the first stone, unless you happen to be a good dancer who loves Barbra Streisand, in which case, step up, and we'll all stone your ass!"

And it would certainly have been no trouble to add, "Oh, yeah, and when I die and there's a religion named after me? Make sure there're no women priests, because I would just hate that, and so would my dad."

I obviously spend way too much time spinning out these kinds of scriptural arguments in my mind. All these years later, I still feel as if I'm in some kind of verbal smackdown with the pope, even though he remains blissfully unaware of it.

Oddly enough, we even have the same publisher now. Recently I was on the phone with my book publisher when all of a sudden I heard her assistant furiously whispering in the background. My editor asked me to hold on a moment, then said quietly to her assistant, "Well, is he calling from Italy?" She murmured something else to her assistant, then got back on the phone.

"Listen, Cathryn, I was wondering if we could continue this after lunch. I'm, well, I'm doing this little book with the pope and . . ."

I couldn't believe it, the pope was calling, the pope was on hold! The pope was waiting for me, endlessly chatty as I am, to get off the goddamned phone! I felt a rush of power as I imagined the pope waiting for me to stop talking. I imagined him impatiently tapping his big signet ring on the phone receiver, absentmindedly playing with his rosary, unhappily listening to an FM lite version of Madonna's "Papa Don't Preach" on the HarperCollins hold music.

I stalled my impeccably polite editor as long as I could, then she eventually dumped me for the head of the Holy Mother Church. When I hung up, I felt a rush of triumph for Denise and me. After all, I had momentarily interfered with the pope's day, and although the victory was petty, it was still sweet.

I still go to church sometimes, but only to the most unbelievably liberal Episcopal Los Angeles church available. A super Grrl Genius friendly church with two women priests, where they call God He or She, depending on the whim of the moment. A church so gay that the one male priest is often not the only man in a dress in the sanctuary on any given Sunday.

Since the Bible still tends to get me worked up, I avoid it and instead read every crackpot inspirational book I can get my hands on. One day, when I was in the Bodhi Tree, a spiritual bookstore in L.A. where you can read for hours and drink all the free herb tea you want, I came across a book that was "staff recommended." It was actually a memoir, but what was inspirational about it was how it had been written.

The book was called *The Diving Bell and the Butterfly,* and it was written by a man who had been the editor of French *Vogue.* He had always wanted to write a book, but then he had this horrifying stroke, and he lost the use of all his human faculties, except that he could blink one eye. Even so, he went ahead and actually wrote his book, by blinking one eye, in code.

Of course I bought the book; I mean, I had to. I realized that the very existence of this book was a triumph of the human spirit, no doubt. Soon, however, I started to realize that the book was also a tragedy for procrastinators everywhere.

The more I thought about it, the more I realized that the Blinky Eye Guy ruins it for everyone, because he has set the bar for overcoming obstacles way too high. Even Stephen Hawking looks like a useless slacker next to this guy.

Say, for example, you were thinking of writing a book, and by *you* I of course mean "me." Maybe you were even going to start writing the book today, but hadn't quite gotten around to it. Maybe you had a terrible hangnail or had eaten some bad clams. These may have seemed like perfectly good excuses until suddenly you'd hear a voice in your head:

"The Blinky Eye Guy gets his stuff in on time! Nobody has to pester the Blinky Eye Guy to turn off *Green Acres* and get to work."

I soon became fixated on the whole idea of the Blinky Eye Guy. I sat around my house, performing time-motion experiments to see how long it would take me to get anything done as a profoundly disabled "wink writer." I soon discovered that it would take well over an hour just to write my name. I started wondering, If this happened to me, would I rise to the occasion? Would I accept this affliction as God's will for me? Or, would I just sit around my house all day blinking, "Fuck you, fuck you, fuck you!"

I talked endlessly to all my friends about my obsession. Other writers had the most sarcastic take on the blinky-eye situation, which I backed 100 percent. My friend Paul, a comedy writer and stay-at-home dad, was completely bitter about the whole thing.

"Oh, sure, the Blinky Eye Guy writes a book, because you know what, the Blinky Eye Guy has all the time in the world," Paul said as he used what looked like a miniature turkey baster to pull a huge wad of snot from his baby's nose.

"I mean look," Paul continued. "The Blinky Eye Guy has somebody wiping his ass, he has someone feeding him intravenously. Like I said, he's got all the time in the world! If I had that kind of time, I'd write a book too."

Paul's wife, Pam, also a comedy writer, a Second Place Live Salad Making winner, and more impressive, a four-time *Jeopardy* champ, was even more caustic. Pam is brilliant and competitive. She doesn't enjoy being outperformed by anyone, certainly not some snooty French guy who writes a book just by batting his pretty little eyes. After having heard an earful on the blinky-eye dilemma from her husband, she called me from her car on the way from a location shoot.

"Hi, it's Pam," she said in her typically rapid-fire way. "Listen, I just heard the Blinky Eye Guy didn't even write the last two chapters of his book. He just had something in his eye."

The cell connection started to break up, but then she came back on to snap at me, "By the way, have you actually read the thing yet?"

I admitted that I hadn't. After all the senseless torture the Blinky Eye Guy had gone through to write his stupid book, I still couldn't manage to get off my ass and actually read the damn thing.

"Well, I read it," she said, "and here's what: it stinks."

Sometimes, when I lose faith in God, all I have to do is look at all the wonderfully sarcastic people I have been lucky enough to know, and I become convinced that there is a God. Only a force of pure love would know that I could never make it through life on earth unless I was surrounded by people as deliciously cynical as my friends. That, plus chocolate and baked goods, is proof enough for me.

Of course, believing in God hasn't stopped me from mostly relying on my own stubborn self-will. Since God has so much on his/her plate, I figure that I'm probably doing him/her a big favor by running my own show as much as possible. I come from a long line of control freaks, and the thought of turning my life and my will over to somebody who keeps allowing Jeff Foxworthy to have sitcoms is some-times more than I can bear.

Thankfully, my absolute faith in God also does not preclude my also having absolute faith in psychics, astrol-ogy, fortune cookies, the *I Ching*, Ouija boards, arcade

Love-O-Meters, Cracker Jack fortunes, or the divine oracle of the Magic 8 Ball.

On and off for a while now, I have been going through what friends politely refer to as "a rough period," which everyone knows really means "her life is completely in the toilet." My marriage had fallen apart, my career seemed stalled, and I was so deeply in debt that I started wondering if working for a live sex chat line would really be all that bad, considering how much I usually enjoy both sex and chat.

I could certainly have relied on my alleged faith in God to pull me though, but that seemed unnecessarily risky. Instead, I headed over to the Psychic Eye on Ventura Boulevard, where the big metal suits of armor and red velvet curtains let you know exactly what kind of cheesy "Love Potion Number Nine" psychic talent you can expect for your $25 an hour.

I had dragged along my friend Ileen, so we could witness each other's session. We made our way through the low-lying fog of patchouli into the darkened private reading room. There we met Felicia, a frighteningly skinny Valley Girl psychic with Raggedy Ann red hair and bad lipliner, who told me, "You need to have, like, more faith in God."

This really frosted my cake, as this was advice I could have gotten for free in any badly lit church basement. She went on to say, "You need to learn how to give up control. You're, like, totally trying to control everything in your life, and since you can't, it's making you superangry. If you stay angry, you're going to get very sick, like you did back in your early twenties, only this time you, like, won't get better."

"What do you mean? Do you mean that I'll, you know, die or something?"

"You totally won't get better" was all that she would say. Now I was terrified. This was not the kind of advice you were supposed to get at the Psychic Eye. They were supposed to tell you that you were going to become a sitcom star and make a lot of money, because that's what most people in L.A. want. In fact, when it was Ileen's turn, Felicia told her that she was going to be on a sitcom and make a lot of money. Which of course turned out to be true, but I didn't know that then.

All the way home from the Psychic Eye I fumed.

"Boy, you'd think if she was so freaking psychic, she'd know that lining your lips like that is so over. Even Susan Lucci gave it up about ten Emmy nominations ago."

Ileen quietly suggested, "Maybe you ought to think about it, the anger thing, the giving-up-control thing, just, you know, for something to think about."

I ignored her and continued on about the bad lip liner. "I mean, seriously, that line was a good two, three inches outside her lips. It looks insane. It looks like she just decided to arbitrarily start drawing red circles around her orifices. Why doesn't she just draw one around her nose, or her—"

"I get it, I get it."

"Every time I see someone with crazy lips like that, I just feel like leaning into their face and ordering myself up a Happy Meal."

I ranted on about the lips like that for the rest of the ride home, sure that this woman's poor taste in grooming was a sign that her dire prediction could be ignored.

But of course, I could not ignore it. As a last, desperate attempt at fixing my life, I prayed. I prayed to God to make everybody shape up and start treating me right. I also prayed to learn how to give up control, if God felt that was really necessary, which it obviously wasn't.

About a month later, I was visiting Ileen and her annoyingly perfect husband in New York City. I was walking along Central Park West on the park side of the street, waiting for a light, when suddenly there was a big yellow taxi speeding directly toward me on the sidewalk.

Time slowed down, my thoughts became clear and focused. My brain was quickly processing the information: "Cab, driving on sidewalk, not good." There was no one else but me on that part of the sidewalk. I was trying to decide if I should jump to the left or the right and was actually praying for God to help me out of this mess, when suddenly it was as if I could see a pair of garishly overlined lips speaking in the proverbial still, small voice.

"Give up control."

The thought didn't seem helpful, and I still hated the way the lips seemed to be mocking me, as though, just because an outline is drawn, I will suddenly be so foolish as to believe that Barbara Hershey thin lips have suddenly become Angelina Jolie thick lips.

"Give up control," insisted the badly lined lips.

Despite the ridiculous overlining, I realized that the lips had a point. Maybe, I thought, what I should do, as this cab is erratically hurtling toward me, is nothing, nothing at all. If I give up control and do nothing, just stand stark still, the driver might be able to see me and steer away. If I jump one way or the other, it might further confuse him, and besides, he's the one with the big yellow taxi, and all I have is a small green chiffon dress. In that fraction of a second, I could see the wisdom of the lips' plan and decided to give up control and do nothing. Except pray.

At the last second, the taxi driver did see me and neatly swerved away, passing by me so close that the yellow of his taxi gently brushed against the chiffon of my dress. He headed to the left, where he finally crunched into the park wall.

I was fine, and the two blue-haired ladies with identical perms in the back of the cab were fine, except one of them was tapping on the driver's window, her little blue poodle head bobbing nervously as she kept asking, "Excuse me. Hello, mister, excuse me, when are we gonna get going again?"

Only in New York is a cabbie who nearly kills you a cabbie you don't want to give up on just quite yet.

All around me, the New Yorkers who are supposedly world famous for not getting involved got very involved. The whole street seemed to swing into action. A rangy, unshaven guy with a guitar on his back pulled the cabbie out of his car and started threatening to hit him over the head with his guitar, screaming, "You could have killed her, you fucking moron. What are you, fucking retarded?"

Two guys in a van pulled over and screamed at me, "Get his number, get his motherfuckin' number!" I stood there like a dullard as someone handed me a pen and paper. I was too jacked up on adrenaline to write coherently, so someone else took the pen and wrote down the cabbie's motherfuckin' number for me.

There, flying on the crack high of my near-death experience, I realized that Manhattan was a blessed, magical island, populated with kind, angelic beings of light. I also realized that I was the recipient of an answered prayer.

I had been made to understand, for an instant, what it was like to trust in my Grrl Genius higher power and to give up control. Unfortunately, almost as soon as I had learned it, I promptly forgot it, and then I tried to remember it again, and that's what I've been doing ever since. At least now I believe that there is a loving God, a personal higher power, who can answer prayers and speaks to each of us directly, whispering the divine truth to us through hideously overlined lips.

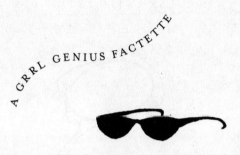

A GRRL GENIUS FACTETTE

*The most frequently sung song
of all time was written by two Grrl Geniuses.*

Mildred Hill and Patty Smith Hill wrote "Happy Birthday to You" in 1893. It was the first song ever sung in outer space (to our knowledge). Every time the song is sung on television or in the movies the foundation set up by those two women receives a royalty, giving new meaning to the phrase "many happy returns."

A GRRL GENIUS LITTLE PINK POST-IT

Hey, Grrl Genius!

Just FYI, some little Grrl Genius facts to cheer you up.

I thought that you should know that Mensa, the international organization of smarty-pants, derives its name from the goddess Mensa, who was the Roman goddess of math.

The three best-selling novels of all time were written by women, Margaret Mitchell, Harper Lee, and Jacqueline Susann

Also, two out of three finalists on the year 2000 *Jeopardy* Teen Tournament of Champions were Grrls.

Grrls rule!

A Grrl Genius Quiz

Find the Grrl Genius Invention.

1. Which of the following was invented by a Grrl Genius:
   A. The fire escape
   B. The bulletproof vest
   C. Pneumatic tires
   D. The dishwasher

2. Which is the Grrl Genius innovation:
   A. The navy's signal flare
   B. The white line in the middle of the road
   C. The circular saw
   D. Disposable diapers

3. Grrl Genius was responsible for which of the following:
   A. Solar heating
   B. Invisible glass
   C. The first causeway system
   D. The ice cream cone

ANSWERS: All of them, Grrl Geniuses invented every last one.

Step Ten

"Continued to Celebrate the Grrl Genius Aging Process"

The great thing about getting older is
you don't lose all the other ages you have been.

—MADELINE L'ENGLE

Age is something that doesn't matter,
unless you are a cheese.

—BILLIE BURKE

To be somebody you must last.

—RUTH GORDON

The real fountain of youth is to have a dirty mind.

—JERRY HALL

It is essential that every Grrl Genius continuously cele-brate the Grrl Genius aging process. If you allow yourself to accept that getting older means you are no longer attrac-tive or valuable, you are doomed. One of the main reasons you can never accept this notion is that "old and ugly" is starting to happen at younger and younger ages.

My sister-in-law Maria recently sent a picture of my gorgeous, brilliant, talented, nine-month-old niece, Maya, to a famous baby photographer. Maria knew the people who published this photographer's art books, and apparently the photographer is always looking for "fresh baby meat." The photographer's "people" returned the snapshot, say-ing that, at nine months and fifteen pounds, Maya was "too old and too fat." She was over-the-hill, used up. She had really let herself go. Apparently, they like the babies to be "incubator thin." Maybe if Maya was willing to "drop two," she would look younger and still have a shot at being a cute baby instead of the faded, decrepit nine-month-old hag she obviously was.

The point is, the way things are going, if nine months is "over-the-hill," then I say the whole concept of over-the-hill needs to be tossed out altogether.

When I think about getting old, I think about Cape Cod, since I'm pretty sure that's where I'd like to end up as the crazy old lady I am sure to become. My family runs a spook house on Cape Cod. I believe that the house is filled with the ghosts of all the crazy old ladies in my family who came before me. It is a big, rambling, crooked beach house bought by my grandfather, a lawyer in Boston. The majority of his clientele had names that involved the use of quotation marks. Names like Larry "the Mole" Benedetti, Dominic "the Squirrel" Pandiani, and my personal favorite, "Hor-rible" Hughes. He took the money he earned freeing the quotation-mark gang from their various legal annoyances and bought the house from a certain Judge Swift.

The house is collectively shared by a number of my aunts and uncles. The inner walls of the house are paper-thin, so that fighting and lovemaking have to be timed around other people's trips to the beach and the store and even the ice cream truck. Although that is rare, because on a hot summer day no one in her right mind chooses quickie sex over a Fudgsicle. The house is crooked and sunken because it actually sits below sea level, and the alleged ground beneath it is really only a marsh of sand and water.

Because of the high water table, the house is part of a community in which the number one topic of conversation is your septic tank. People pray nightly for the holy grail of sewerage. The larger town refuses to run the sewer system out to this community because, after all, almost everyone there is just "summer people." This battle of the sewerage has been raging for the last fifty years.

Septic systems constantly fail, due to the high water table, which causes people in our small beach town to spend far too much time pondering their own effluvia. In the annual children's Fourth of July parade, tiny children are dressed as septic tanks and made to carry signs that read "Make Our #2 Your #1 Priority."

When people in New Silver Beach talk about dealing with their own shit, they are not speaking metaphorically. Our next-door neighbors, who live here year-round, finally gave up on the impossible dream of a sewer and spent $20,000 to build a twelve-foot-aboveground title-five septic tank, which has become a kind of second-story backyard where they happily sit on top of their own waste products and have a perfect view of the ocean.

So septically obsessed are people on Cape Cod that there is a performance artist in Providence who has recently built a performance space in an old septic tank on his property called The Septic Space.

For me, growing up, the effect of all this community

excremental fixation usually resulted in severe constipation. I was terrified to use the bathroom in our house. Since you never knew when the "system" was going to back up, I began to worry that I would be responsible for the fatal flush that would shut down the house in the middle of the summer fun.

I believe that the ghosts that haunt this house are swimming around in the emotional cesspool that burbles and gurgles beneath this house. The past becomes as impossible to ignore as our own fecal matter. The longstanding argument that ruins the family clambake is as sudden and yet inevitable as the overflowing toilet. In this house I have learned, on a tangible level, that if you don't deal with your own shit, it will surely come back to haunt you.

If I do become a crazy old lady on Cape Cod, I will surely take up the mantle of the sewer wars and fight to the very end for the right to have my waste products chemically treated by the State of Massachusetts.

Our beach house was probably bought not with my grandfather's ill-gotten, second-tier-Mafia legal fees, but with family money. His parents were slumlords in Boston, and buying and ruining real estate was a family tradition. Family legend was that my great-grandparents had sewn jewels into the linings of their sable coats when they had come from Russia to America.

My great-aunt Miriam was said to still have "the family jewels," not in the gonadal sense but in the actual gem version. Miriam was a fantastic old lady who had no problem embracing aging. She was a Grrl Genius poet and an activist who slept with Arthur Fiedler and Carl Sandburg. Actually, I don't know for sure about the sleeping part, but judging from the correspondence, I'm confident that there was at least heavy napping.

It was said that Miriam kept the family diamonds in a safe-deposit box in a bank in Cambridge and then, as a typical Yankee, raised a fuss when the rate on the box was upped $5 a year. She was well-known in Cambridge due to her dowager's hump and community activism. There were reports that she made loud protestations in the bank that she "certainly wasn't going to keep her valuable jewels in a bank run by thieving, larcenous usury mongers."

So she took her jewels with great fanfare and was robbed three days later in her million-dollar Cambridge house that was falling down from disrepair, the house itself a testament to the very dear cost of saving so much money. She died in that house of the osteoporosis that has me chugging calcium horse pills daily. She died alone, in the bath, in a house that by then was probably only being held up by the newspapers that were stacked ceiling high, crazy-person style, in many of its rooms. When she died, my mother, the neat and organized "white sheep" of her messy lunatic parents, went through every inch of that Cambridge house, as if it were Olduvai Gorge, archaeologically sifting through the layers. She would go through piles of newspapers and find a bankbook with fifty grand in it from 1943, or the skeleton of a long-dead cat, or a handwritten note from Carl Sandburg.

My aunt Miriam was a Grrl Genius just the same. She lived her life according to her own rules. She went to Harvard when it was still Radcliffe. She studied what she wanted, and she wrote what she wanted, and she had affairs with whom she wanted, and she kept all the newspapers she wanted, and goddamnit, if she didn't want to pay five bucks more a year to store her diamonds, well, that was her prerogative. She was one of those women who transcended her lack of physical beauty to become something much more interesting. She wasn't beautiful, she was fascinating. And you can't minimize her lack of looks. She wasn't "plain" or "unfussy" or the ultimate backward compliment that is always doled out to ugly women, "handsome."

To begin with, she had an enormous Quasimodo hump, but that was just the appetizer course of her cosmetic defects. She had a Toucan Sam beak of a nose and a mustache with all the lushness one would expect from Tom Selleck or some other eighties action hero. She had squinty, beady, little eyes and the kind of moles that are so large you begin to wonder if she was one of those people who was genetically meant to be twins or triplets, and if maybe the moles on her face were the fetal heads of her own absorbed siblings, complete with long, flowing hair.

She was ugly enough to scare small children, and I know this for a fact because I was one of them. She knew she scared people. She would wait for you to recover from the initial shock, then she would help you get over your inherent shallowness until you fully absorbed the beauty of her soul.

The older she got, the uglier she got, and she could not have cared less. Her profoundly gruesome appearance didn't seem to bother her one bit, which is a feat of genius few women ever approach. Certainly not the movie stars and supermodels who worry about their cellulite daily, hourly, moment to moment, along with the rest of us.

Miriam was always referred to as a spinster. It was clear from the adults that her ugliness and aloneness were meant to serve as a warning. On the surface, her life seemed pretty great to me, but clearly you were supposed to feel sorry for her, because she was alone, because she didn't have children. What was unclear was whether she became ugly because she chose to be alone, or whether she had to be alone because she was so ugly.

I felt much more sorry for my grandmother Ida, a clearly brilliant woman who was forced to put her brain on a shelf and attempt to raise five children she obviously didn't want as she endured my grandfather's endless abusive tirades. My grandmother was beautiful, had a family and nice homes, but she was the one I felt sorry for. She had made herself small, minimized her talents so that everyone else would feel okay. The way I saw it, Aunt Miriam had it made. Sure, she looked like a witch, but like all witches, her magic was clearly ample compensation for her ugliness.

There have been a lot of beautiful women in Cambridge, but people there still remember my aunt Miriam, because she was fascinating. She was that rare adult to whom you could say "I think I'd like to win a Tony Award" and she would say that was a splendid idea. Not because she was patronizing you, but because she didn't see any reason why you shouldn't. She was an OGG, Original Grrl Genius.

In his own twisted way her brother Morris, my grandfather, could be considered an Enlightened Male. Whereas Ida was terrified of aging and dedicated her life to minimizing herself with relentless dieting and the constant denial of her vast intelligence, Morris dedicated his life to being large. He lifted weights and smoked cigars and yelled, so that his sound and scent filled the beach house and even spilled out onto the street. He was an emotional tyrant and a relentless, alcoholic bully. He scarred his own children so deeply that even though he has been dead for fifteen years, my uncles still call each other deep into sleepless nights and ask, "Is he still dead?"

My grandfather was also a Damon Runyonesque lech. When I was fifteen, standing in the kitchen of the ramshackle beach house in my bikini, he growled to me, "Ya got nice stems!"

I had no idea what he was talking about and I asked him what he had said, and even more irate, he spat out, "Ya got nice stems! Gams, stems, ya got a nice ass fer crissakes!" Well, I knew what that meant, and I knew it wasn't the kind of compliment Grandpa Walton or Mr. Rogers or Mr. French or any of the other nice old men on TV handed out, so I kept it to myself.

My grandfather looked like a mafioso. He deliberately cultivated this look with his cigar smoking and weight lifting and his insistence on always traveling with his violin case. I mean, he was an actual violinist, so the violin case wasn't a total affectation. Still, he had seen all those old Hollywood gangster movies and knew that a guy in a trench coat and sunglasses with a stogie and a violin case is not going to be taken for a musician, he is going to be mistaken for a gangster, which is exactly the effect he was going for. The joke was even more hilarious at airport security when they would do a hand check of his "violin case" and he would whip off a quick rendition of Bach's "Chacon."

He handed out verbal abuse and twenty-dollar bills in equally generous amounts and taught me the whole concept of racial prejudice through a series of dirty jokes and vicious screeds filled with epithets that weren't part of normal conversation back in liberal Lutheran Minnesota. In fact, even though I grew up surrounded by Swedish people, it wasn't until I actually married one that I knew that Swedes were called "Squareheads."

Despite the hatred my grandfather displayed toward entire groups of people because of their ethnicity, not to be confused with the specific hatreds he doled out to family and friends, the one thing he never did was say that women were less qualified or intelligent than men. His own marriage reminded me of those stories you hear of World War II soldiers who are trapped on a Pacific island, guerrillas fighting each other into old age because no one has bothered to tell them that the war is, in fact, over. Even so, his wife, after forty years in the marital trenches, finally went back to law school and eventually became the oldest person in Massachusetts ever to pass the bar. Remarkably, it was the one thing he never gave her any shit about. In the most twisted way possible, I have to award him the title of Enlightened Male, even if it is on a technicality.

My father, like my grandfather, is allowed to be large; his personality is enormous, and entertaining. At the dinner table he tells wonderful long stories in which he is always the hero. The stories are usually about flying small airplanes, which was his job at one point in his life. In the stories, there is often a sudden squall and a failure of equipment, and through skill and cunning and sheer nerve he manages to save our family from certain death in a single-engine plane as we narrowly avoid the "rock-filled cloud" of a mountain. The point of the story is always that my father is brilliant and clever and brave. The idea that perhaps personal aviation is a recklessly dangerous hobby that you shouldn't foist on your unsuspecting family is never the point of the story.

My mother has definitely followed in the family female tradition of downplaying her obvious gifts. My mother's brilliance is by necessity quieter; she is the one who silently sits at the kitchen counter on Sunday afternoon and easily fills out the *New York Times* crossword puzzle in ink, as if it were a DMV form. I remember when I was little, she would iron my dad's shirts as she watched *Jeopardy,* softly answering every single question. The hiss of the Niagara spray starch would sizzle under the hot weight of the iron as she murmured, "Who are the Etruscans?" "What is the War of the Roses?" "What is the Strait of Juan de Fuca?" I remember thinking, Dad can't do that, so why doesn't he have to iron the shirts?

My friend Pam has remarked on the foolhardiness of anyone who would dare to underestimate my mother. When noting my mother's remarkable cataloging of the many gourmet recipes she effortlessly prepares, Pam encouragingly suggests that my mom "really ought to write a cookbook," not knowing that she has, in fact, written several. My mom is the sort of person who, when she isn't studying Chinese (Mandarin) or making origami dragons,

likes to kick it out on the back porch while sipping hot tea
and idly mapping the human genome.

Every summer our family left our Gulag home in Minnesota and spent three weeks "back East." We would bask in
the gentle, warm waters of Cape Cod and spend a few glit-
tering days in New York City. It was as if those three weeks
just served as a reminder of how miserable the other forty-
nine weeks were going to be among the dour, white, taci-
turn Lutherans of Roseville. Every delicious bowl of clam
chowder only served as a reminder of the "beer cheese"
soup that awaited us back on the prairie. Beer cheese soup
is a soup in which the title ingredients are the only ingredients; it's a gelatinous mélange of Velveeta and beer. It is
basically soup made out of what can be scraped off the floor
of any lakeside bar in northern Minnesota. New England
clam chowder consists of the fruits of the sea blended with
onions and spices and care, it is a symphony of delicate flavors, whereas beer cheese soup is a dial tone of two hideous
flavors, whose blending only serves to bring out each
other's vile, rank, bar-floor-like qualities.

My three weeks back East every year convinced me that
I was being held hostage in a horrible Archipelago. I iden-
tified with Alexander Solzhenitzyn far more than any
grade-school Grrl ought to. I dreamt of escaping Minnesota, where people said things like "Oh fer cute" and
insisted on calling their bathrooms "the Biffy," and where
it was so cold then when you stepped out the front door in
the morning, the mucous membranes in your nose froze so
solidly that you could hear the echo of them crackling
loudly inside your head as they hardened.

Minnesota was not only dull, it was dangerous. At
recess, we were forced to play outside unless it was fifteen
degrees below zero or lower, and that was the actual tem-
perature, not windchill. Some days, walking home from
school, I remember feeling sleepy and thinking that I

would love to curl up and take a nap in the snow; of course I know now that this was the latter stages of hypothermia. Dull yellow patches of frostbite regularly graced our wrists. Recreation consisted of loading helpless children onto school buses and taking us to two giant hills that had been sprayed down with fire hoses until they were as hard and slick as Pamela Anderson Lee's original *Baywatch* implants.

We were then inserted into giant inner tubes and hurled recklessly down the frozen mammary mountains. Injuries were regular and expected; the unforgiving ice was covered with giant slicked-over red patches of blood, small reminders of previously busted teeth, noses, and collar-bones. Another favorite neighborhood activity was broom ball. Armies of small kids and their older Hamm's-beer-fueled siblings would put on rubber boots and run around on yet another blood-splattered ice rink, viciously whack-ing a tetherball with duct-taped kitchen brooms, a savage form of recreation that freed you from the relative safety and gentility of hockey.

Minnesota was trying to kill me. I had to get out. Also, I wanted to be famous and I knew that no one really famous is from Minnesota. There's F. Scott Fitzgerald, but he got out, and he had the good grace never to mention the place. You didn't see the great Gatsby slurping beer cheese soup or playing Daisy in broom ball. There's Garrison Keillor, but, God bless him, he has about as much pizzazz as Lurch from the Addams family. Then of course there's always Prince, but Prince would be famous in Minnesota no mat-ter what he did, because he's the black guy. People there don't even know he's a musician, they just say, "Oh, we just love that Prince, he's the black guy, you know."

My escape from Minnesota to New York became a real possibility in fourth grade when my best friend Nancy Schmaedeke's mom pulled me aside to give me a dire warn-ing about our local mall, Har Mar Mall. She said, "Now,

Cathy, I don't want you girls going alone into those bathrooms at Har Mar Mall, okay? Because there are terrible men there, who will grab you. Those men will grab you and they will inject you with a serum and put you in a burlap bag and kidnap you to New York City, where you'll be sold into prostitution on Minnesota Strip. Because they like little blond girls in New York City."

All I heard from this dire tale was "New York City!" Oh, how I longed to be injected with the serum and put into the bag and transported to that island of splendor. I had no idea what prostitution was, but if it got me out of Roseville, Minnesota, I was all for it.

In New York City, I would be a glamorous Broadway star, acting, singing, and writing my way into the hearts of the people. I would be large, like the men in my family, like Aunt Miriam. I would know famous, brilliant people and I would tell exciting, partially true stories at dinner in which I would be the heroine. I would have a splendid pied-à-terre apartment, which from my study of French I knew meant "foot on dirt," but I was sure it was nicer than it sounded. When I had a little downtime from being the toast of the town, I would take the *New York Times* up to the beach house on Cape Cod for the weekend, where I would quickly fill out the puzzle in ink and try desperately not to have a bowel movement so as not to ruin the relative septic serenity.

My plan was to grow old but remain fabulous and accomplished. I would be a true Grrl Genius, bragging about myself and others. What I didn't realize is that regardless of what efforts I made, eventually, like Aunt Miriam, I would be considered ugly. The way society sees it, eventually every woman who lives past seventy is ugly. Brigitte Bardot is wrongly considered faded, desiccated, and, yes, ugly. If Brigitte Bardot is ugly, I will surely be ghastly, so I better just get ready for it.

In living the Grrl Genius philosophy, I am able not just

to accept but embrace this inevitable so-called ugliness. It will be a welcome relief after a lifetime of trying to be cute. I often fantasize about what my crazy-old-lady look will be, even going so far as developing a series of paper dolls that allow me to decide whether my look will be focused around giant picture hats or enormous, garishly colored scarves or pounds and pounds of Kenneth Jay Lane rhinestone jewelry.

A few years ago, when I wrote a humor book about Jane Austen, I was asked to speak at the Beverly Hills Ladies Auxiliary Book Club Luncheon, a fantastic nirvana of crazy-old-lady couture and attitude.

The club is run by a brilliant literary diva, Mrs. Edna Williamson. She wears gold-lamé pajamas and a giant, sweeping blond updo and crimson red lipstick, which she smears liberally over the general vicinity of her mouth. She is a teacher of elocution to the young ladies of Beverly Hills, particularly the Farsi-speaking young ladies of Beverly Hills. After lunch is served, she performs, with Mr. Andre at the piano, a five-minute, one-woman version of a classic American musical comedy, even though she cannot sing a note. Like Aunt Miriam, she is fascinating, she is a Grrl Genius. She is large, yea, she contains multitudes.

I have spent a lot of time sitting in the family beach house, trying to keep my fiber consumption down and thinking about what my crazy-old-lady act will be. So far I have it that I dress all in black, but I have giant tufts of cat hair that float lazily across my shrunken breasts as if they were tumbleweeds and my wizened chest were their geriatric O.K. Corral. I wear lipstick, but I don't even think of confining it to one mere facial orifice; the scarlet swath angles lazily up to my nostrils and stretches to my ears as I gleefully decorate my face like a daring cubist painter.

My act involves trained seals, which I keep in the harbor near the beach house. Together, the seals and I perform modern dance to the theme songs from the Sherwood Schwartz oeuvre of television shows, particularly *Gilligan's Island* and *The Brady Bunch*.

I think about perfecting my old-lady act because it keeps me from panicking about the present. In the present, I am separated from my husband, trying to figure out what to do about this marriage here in the house where I got engaged, and where my parents met each other, and where my grandparents spent a lifetime living like emotional ninja warriors.

I sit on the beach with my beautiful cousin Jen, a sometimes model who was always told she was "the ugly one," a graduate student at Harvard who was always told she was "the stupid one." The tradition of keeping the women in my family small continues.

Jen is living in Boston with a tattooed, Irish gourmet chef. She is trying to decide if they should should stay together. They want to relocate, but she isn't sure that where he wants to go will be good for her career as an art historian. I tell her that you can't make yourself small for another person, you can't hide your fabulousness to make your partner feel more fabulous. If he doesn't worship, or at the very least accommodate, your genius, he's not the guy for you. That is the Grrl Genius code.

I realize that what I'm telling her is exactly what I need to hear. Can my marriage accommodate my bigger ambitions? Maybe my husband deserves to be with someone less ambitious, someone who isn't so ambivalent about having children, about living simply. I know I can't pretend to want these things just because it will make him happy.

I have become obsessed with this idea of the various ways that potential Grrl Geniuses have allowed themselves to be made small throughout history. In ancient China, women's feet were bound tightly from the time they were small children, the feet atrophying, the bones becoming gnarled and fused and the flesh eventually putrefying, thus creating the ideal lotus-blossom foot. Helpless and unable to walk, the more deformed and crippled the woman, the more erotic she became.

People are messed up about feet to this day. I know this from my time spent as a runway shoe model in Chicago. Shoe buyers would try to pick you up by complimenting your feet. They would remark on the highness of my arch, or my fantastic "toe cleavage" as I hobbled around in spiked shoes I was told to say were "unbelievably comfortable."

As a Grrl Genius, I can choose to wear any shoe I want, and I often choose something chunky and open-toed. No foot binder comes and forces me into it, and so I think that's fine. But I have often made the mistake of binding my own ambitions or dreams or feelings until they become gnarled and putrefied and small. No one has done that to me, I do it to myself.

My grandmother Ida kept herself small except at the very end of her life. After she became a lawyer, my grandmother lived only a few more years. Ida died in her sixties of colon cancer. I wonder if she, like me, sat in this beach house and tried to will her body from voiding its wastes so as not to cause a fuss.

I have idolized Aunt Miriam's spinsterhood, but maybe I have minimized the impact of years of people feeling sorry for you because you are old and ugly and alone. I wonder if maybe she wasn't quite as large as I imagined, if maybe she was slightly less sure of the value of being her own person toward the end of her long life. She died of osteoporosis, the dowager's hump she carried for years. It was almost as if the force of the family ethic of female inferiority, this family "peer pressure," finally made itself known on a physical level in her body. Her spine became a weird sort of "antirack," softening and curling in on itself, conspiring against her will, and the largeness of her personality, to try to make her small after all. Gradually, her body became so hunched over that her internal organs began to be crushed. Eventually, her entire body suffered the fate of the Chinese noblewoman's desiccated foot. Becoming smaller than you are supposed to be will kill you. It killed Aunt Miriam, and on some level it is killing me.

So Jen and I sit on the beach and try to figure out how not to get small, how to be Grrl Geniuses and how to love ourselves for our genius, how to celebrate our Grrl Genius aging process, even if we end up old and weird and alone.

Jen and I agree, in true Grrl Genius fashion, that the best way to do this is not to try to solve our personal problems, but to figure out what our crazy-old-lady drag will be, and to work up our act. When asked to think of the main, signature feature of her crone drag, Jen comes up with the idea of "wacky headbands." When I suggest that she may be thinking small, she ups the ante to tiaras, a far more appropriate choice. Inspired by her, I abandon picture hats and make the bold leap to gold, jeweled turbans. I am cheating slightly because my yoga teacher is an American Sikh who wears a turban, and so I am privy to the knowledge that they are not only attention-getting, but they also provide a cheap and pain-free face-lift effect as well.

Jen and I decide that we will be crazy old ladies who live in Manhattan and on Cape Cod. We agree that we will be wacky, octogenarian performance artists. We will call ourselves The Crazy Old Ladies. The way Jen and I figure it, if you're going to be a great crazy old lady, you can't go halfway.

The following is a review of our act that will appear in the *Cape Cod Tribune* in June of 2050, by which time Jen and I will be what we prefer to think of as ripe Grrl Geniuses and what the world will probably still refer to as ugly. They will be wrong to think so because, in fact, we will be brilliant and talented and better than beautiful. We will be fascinating.

Cape Cod Tribune

ARTS AND LEISURE SECTION

Weekend Best Bet for Entertainment!

"THE CRAZY OLD LADIES" ARE A TRIUMPH IN A RETURN ENGAGEMENT

By Willey Lovell

This weekend heralds the return of the *grandes dames* of Cape Cod glitterati, those cunning cousines Jen Watson and Cathryn Michon, better known as The Crazy Old Ladies. They are premiering their new performance work, *Flush Proudly*, at the world-famous Septic Space Opera House in Provincetown.

The piece is a delightful mélange of music, dance, and trapeze artistry. Miss Michon and Miss Watson are accompanied by the Septic Orchestra, featuring world-renowned percussionist Reza Contrero on copper pipes and low-flush toilets. As usual, the coy cousins are also joined by the Gay Male Chorus of Provincetown, who do spectacular double duty as singers and sedan-chair carriers.

In the first movement Miss Michon, in a four-foot, golden turban that is held steady by two of the Province-town chanteurs, performs a delightful Balinese shadow-puppet spectacle that depicts five generations of petty arguments at family clambakes revolving around the best ways to avoid having the cesspool pumped.

The second movement features Miss Watson in her signature tiara and little else, performing a Fluxus-inspired installation entitled "Turd Eater." In this portion of the evening Miss Watson sits center stage, surrounded by large mounds of chocolate fudge (provided by the ever-popular Kopper Kettle on Main Street in Cotuit). She proceeds symbolically, almost eucharistically, to eat the fudge. After a while she begins to demand that members of the audience take part in her ritualistic feast, dramatically forcing the audience to join her in this, the ultimate act of self-acceptance. Fortunately for the audience, the fudge is delightfully rich and surprisingly low in calories.

The evening ends on a high note as Les Cousines Anciennes delightfully warble a plaintive duet calling out to their dead ancestors who haunt the still-teeming septic system beneath their shoreline home. The Crazy Old Ladies beseech their long-gone relatives to stop haunting the tank, tell them to end their futile vigil of waiting for the city sewer pipes that will never come. Miss Michon and Miss Watson, along with the chorus, then perform a final swirling dance involving yards and yards of white-sequined toilet paper, and a remarkable number of well-endowed, young, naked men, as they triumphantly sing of their decision to love themselves fully by flushing proudly, the consequences be damned.

I highly recommend *Flush Proudly*. This landmark performance, followed perhaps by a late-night hot fudge sundae at the Kopper Kettle, gives you all the makings of a perfect Cape Cod evening. The superb artistry, coupled with this powerful and timely message of bodily self-love, makes this an evening in the theater this reviewer will not soon forget.

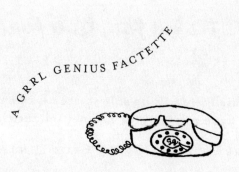

A GRRL GENIUS FACTETTE

Grrl Geniuses get the hiccups
one-quarter as often as men.

The Grrl Genius Craft Project

In which you will be able to create a paper-doll-type refrigerator magnet set entitled:

"CREATE YOUR GRRL GENIUS 'CRAZY OLD LADY' LOOK"

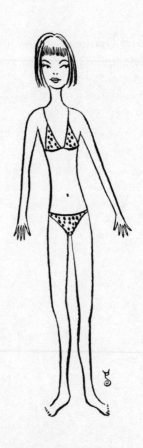

Cut out
for face...

Red Cape

Silk Kimono

Real
Chanel Suit

Purple & Turquoise
Velvet Lounging
Pyjamas

pink
High tops

Big Floppy
Hat

Big Weird
Scarf

Tiara

Tangly
Bracelet

Cleopatra Wig

Jeweled
Turban

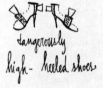

dangerously
high-heeled shoes

A GRRL GENIUS LITTLE PINK POST-IT

Hey, Grrl Genius!

How many times have you heard that men and women are the way they are because it's been that way since "caveman days." This theory, popular with noted big fat idiot Rush Limbaugh, postulates that cavemen went out and slaughtered animals, and because the men got all the food and had all the power, they were allowed to drag the women back to the cave by their hair and boss them around. According to this lame-ass theory, cavemen were sexy because they were real men, who wore totally hot leather thongs, and cavewomen were inferior and knew their place.

Any amateur anthropologist who tries to sell you this story is confusing "caveman days" with "trailer-park days."

Enlightened Male anthropologist Ashley Montague points out that these societies should actually be referred to as "gatherer-hunter" societies, because it was the gathering that provided 80 percent of their nutrition. The occasional steak was certainly welcome, but without the nuts and berries, cavepeople were screwed, and cavemen knew it.

What's great to know about "caveman days" is that for

possibly as long as sixty thousand years of human prehis-
tory, societies existed in what anthropologist Grrl
Genius Riane Eisler calls "partnership model" societies.
Men and women were equally revered, they worshiped
male gods and female goddesses, the idols they worshiped were not overly skinny, and nobody bossed anyone around too much because everyone was valuable and
important.

The oppression of women as second-class citizens has
been going strong only for about twenty-five hundred
years of human existence, give or take five hundred
years. Apparently for sixty thousand years we actually had
it right. If you reduce the numbers and think of
humankind as being thirty years old, that means we've
basically been in a bad relationship for 1.25 years, a little over a year, and, hey, it's time to break up. Think of
this twenty-five-hundred-year period as one alcoholic
college boyfriend who listens to Guns N' Roses obsessively, and get over it. Who can't get over a crummy year-
long relationship? Who doesn't hate Guns N' Roses?

The truth is that cavemen were sexy, incredibly sexy.
They were sexy because they understood that cavegrrls
were Grrl Geniuses, that God isn't a big bossy white guy,
and that nobody has the right to drag anybody around by
the hair. Plus the totally hot leather thongs.

Emma Thompson

A GRRL GENIUS PROFILE IN EXCELLENCE

(Also a shameless way of sucking up to a celebrity
I would give anything to meet)

Emma Thompson is one of the most talented people working in feature films in this or any century. If her Grrl Genius were limited just to the subtle, luminous screen acting she is most commonly known for, that would be enough to make her a world-class Grrl Genius.

However, Emma's genius only begins with her acting. She was also an amazingly hilarious stand-up comic, sketch performer, and writer back in England.

Also, her Grrl Genius sense of style is witty, elegant, and fun. She showed her breasts in a movie. They were real and really beautiful.

As if that weren't enough, she is also a (deservedly) Oscar-winning screenwriter. With her astoundingly perfect adaptation of *Sense and Sensibility*, she brilliantly brought the Grrl Genius of Über Grrl Genius Jane Austen to millions of people around the world.

Plus, what about how sweet she is to her mom, the wonderful actress Phyllida Law? Emma and her momma could not have been more adorable at the Oscars together if they tried.

Additionally, Emma Thompson, for all her accomplishments and accolades, seems like exactly the sort of person with whom you would love to spend an afternoon having tea and passionately discussing the brilliant writing of Jane Austen.

Emma Thompson is exactly the sort of person with whom *I* would like to spend an afternoon having tea and passionately discussing the brilliant writing of Jane Austen.

Emma Thompson, I love you, and your Grrl Genius!

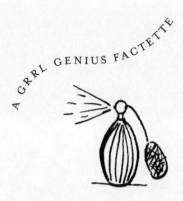

A GRRL GENIUS FACTETTE

The devil was invented to persecute Grrl Geniuses.

In medieval times, the cult of Mary was gaining popularity and church elders were threatened by this newly powerful goddess figure, so they literally invented "the devil," a concept that had not existed in any previous civilization. The idea that one singular evil being was responsible for all things despicable in the world had never been popular. Women were said to be particularily vulnerable to the devil and his minions. The physical manifestation of this new devil included a host of images and symbols that had traditionally been associated with goddess worship. The color red, the horns, the cloven hooves, the trident—all these were pagan goddess images. The devil was then pimped out to be the primary mover and shaker behind persecution of "witches" (any interesting woman, i.e., a Grrl Genius). These Grrl Genius "witches" were then tortured and burned by the millions.

Thus was born the phrase "the devil made me do it."

Not all that funny, but unfortunately, true.

Step Eleven

"We're Entirely Ready to Love the First Grrl Genius We Ever Met, Our Mother"

The mother is the most precious possession of the nation, so precious that society advances its highest well-being when it protects the functions of the mother.

—ELLEN KEY

The phrase "working mother" is redundant.

—JANE SELLMAN

The way to keep children at home is to make home a pleasant atmosphere—and to let the air out of the tires.

—DOROTHY PARKER

My mother believes in always having a good breakfast. Breakfast at my mother's house is usually eggs and toast and homemade jam and fresh-squeezed orange juice, with pretty dishes and cut-crystal jam pots and place mats and nice silver, and that's not just on special occasions.

I do not always have a good breakfast, unless you consider stale M&M's fished out from the lint and grit in the bottom of my purse a "good breakfast." Don't get me wrong, once you wipe them off, they're good, they're just not a "good breakfast."

On the day I filed for my divorce, I decided to have a "good breakfast."

My mother never filed for divorce, but I feel certain that if she had, she'd have had a good breakfast before she headed off to the lawyer's office.

To get my predivorce good breakfast, I went to the ultragroovy Urth Café, where supermodels in yoga-wear sip chai tea and worry about how fat they are. Due to my chronic, incurable tendency to be late, my good breakfast was eaten L.A.-style, "to go."

In all the great cities of the world, there are specific styles of dining. In Paris, impossibly chic people sit at outdoor cafés eating and having deep discussions as they smoke their heads off. The festive native custom of L.A. is dashboard dining, eating meals and ingesting beverages as you talk on the phone and operate heavy machinery that is hurtling through space at life-threatening speeds.

My mother does not eat and drive, but I have eaten more meals at the wheel than I have at my dining room table. I once saw in the Lillian Vernon catalog a little table that fit over your steering wheel, a little dashboard dining-room table. I was so excited that I would finally have some gracious living at last. I imagined my little table with a lovely little linen tablecloth, maybe even tiny little candelabra for evening. I was going to buy it, except that I could never figure out how the little table would stay horizontal when you turned the wheel. My dashboard dinette set would be great for eating four-course meals while driving through the Mojave desert, but not so good for eating sushi while driving through the Hollywood hills, so I abandoned the dream.

My good breakfast on the morning of my divorce was a latte and a muffin. As I waited in line at the crowded counter, my cell phone rang. It was one of my two friends named Pam, Pam T. She had called to see how I was doing, knowing that today I was filing for divorce. I then proceeded to discuss my personal problems in front of a roomful of strangers.

My mother would never discuss her personal problems in front of a roomful of strangers. My mother doesn't really discuss her personal problems at all.

"So today's the day?" Pam T. asked gently.

"Yeah. It's tough, and God knows, I'll miss the sex," I blithely announced to the assembled throng at the café. "He's going to meet me at the lawyer's office, so I don't have to, you know, file alone."

"Well, that's really decent of him."

"I know, I think so too. I mean, he showed up for the wedding, and now he's showing up for the divorce. Who knows, maybe we'll finally be able to get along if we're not married. Oh, hang on, I have to order."

I turned to the swarthy, handsome man behind the counter. "Hi, um, I'll have a decaf, nonfat, large, Italia latte, and a nonfat cranberry-pumpkin muffin, to go."

"Well, somebody is taking care of herself, isn't she?" Pam T. cooed.

Now done with ordering, I launched directly back into my trauma. "I just can't believe how much it hurt to tell him I wanted the divorce. I mean, it was the second time I told him, and it hurt just as bad as the first time."

"I can imagine," Pam T. murmured.

"I guess it's like being shot."

"What's that supposed to mean?" she asked, understandably confused.

"Well, I was thinking about it. I mean, if you get shot, it really hurts."

"Right," she intoned warily, sure there must be more.

"But if you get better, and then you get shot again, it hurts just as bad. Some things are just painful no matter what. Getting shot hurts; every time you get shot, it hurts the same as the last time you were shot."

Pam T. sounded worried. "Why are you so obsessed with being shot? Have you ever been shot?"

"No, I've never been shot, that's not the point."

By this time I had gotten my latte, but I had been so lost in my gunshot/divorce analogy that I realized the guy behind the counter had forgotten to get me my muffin.

"Pam, can you hold on, I didn't get my muffin." She stayed on the line as I turned to the sweet counter guy. I knew his English, although good, was not perfect, so I slowly overenunciated my request in the time-honored style of imperialists everywhere.

"Excuse me, I had a muffin? A cranberry-pumpkin muffin?"

"Yohan," he replied.

Assuming that yohan was Spanish for muffin, I tried to elaborate. "Yes, right, it was cranberry pumpkin, *cran-ber-ry pump-kin?"*

"Yohan," he insisted.

Fine, fine, don't assimilate, I thought. What's it to me? Come to America, serve up all the muffins you like, and then insist on calling them *yohans.* Go ahead, I couldn't care less as long as you just get me my cranberry-pumpkin *yohan muy pronto por favor!*

I didn't say that of course; instead I said, "I'm sorry, I

just, I'm in a little bit of a hurry, so if I could just get the cranberry-pumpkin muffin, or *yohan,* or whatever, please?"

"Yohan," he maddeningly repeated, pointing at me. "It's in yo'han'."

It was then that I noticed he was pointing at my hand, or "yohan" as he knew it. The fucking muffin had been clutched in my greedy little hand the whole time.

"The fucking muffin is in my hand!" I yelled into the phone.

From the other end I heard Pam T.'s endless, hiccupy laughter.

My mother speaks many languages and would surely have known that *yohan* is not Spanish for muffin, that there is in fact no Spanish word for muffin at all. *Pan dulce,* which literally means "sweet bread," is the closest they come.

Furthermore, my cranberry-pumpkin *yohan* was inedible, due to it's low-fatness. The Spanish-speaking peoples have no word for low-fat muffins, but they do have a name for the foolish white people who order them: *"los gringos estúpidos."*

I am a *"gringa estúpida"* from time to time, and being able to admit that is part of my Grrl Genius. It is one of the many charming foibles that makes up my genius. Everyone knew that Einstein couldn't drive, which seems kind of stupid, and yet that only enhanced his reputation as a genius. I can not only drive, but I can drive and talk on the phone and eat a meal and apply makeup all at the same time. I just didn't know that *yohan* is not Spanish for muffin. Hence, I, like Einstein, am a genius.

Anyone who questions my mother's genius is a fool. Forget about her knowledge of history or Latin or Greek or any of the many languages, including Mandarin Chinese, that she has learned. My mother's genius is best explained by the fact that when I was in grade school and wanted an Easy-Bake washer to go with my Easy-Bake oven, my mother "allowed" me to use the real washer and had me doing all the laundry for a couple of months.

Now that's genius.

On the day I filed for divorce, I scheduled my time as though it were any other day. Which means I was late for everything. I was late for my lunch meeting, and late to the lawyer's office. Since I had been late for my wedding, it's not that surprising that I was late for my divorce. As I made my way to the lawyer's office, trapped in glacial, snarled traffic, I pounded the wheel and swore.

"Fuck, fuck, fuck, fuck, fuck!"

My mother does not swear. In fact, my mother is like the spell check on my computer: she simply doesn't acknowledge swear words that she has heard thousands of times. Whenever my computer's spell check sees *fuck,* it automatically suggests *frock* or *fork* or *folk* . My mother would happily second all of these suggestions.

However, "Fork, frock, folk, frock, fork!" is nowhere near as satisfying, despite that both my mother and my computer seem to prefer it.

The real truth is that I think my mother likes it when I swear; I think it's somewhat cathartic for her. I think there are a lot of things she'd like to swear about, and so I am her swearing proxy. I swear a lot because I'm swearing for two.

I think swearing and using slang are important for the whole Grrl Genius movement, because words can be weapons unless you claim them and define them for yourself. When the rap group Prodigy came out with their hit single "Smack My Bitch Up!" a lot of people got pissed, or as my computer alternatively suggests, *poised, posed, passed,* or *kissed.*

The song was banned from Kmart, and the leader of the group defended it, saying that all the controversy was bullshit *(bullish, bellyache, belch).* He said the song wasn't about hitting women at all. He said that "smack my bitch up" was just an expression, that meant doing something intensely creative, such as performing onstage. Or writing a book. I'm smacking my bitch up black and blue even as we speak.

I know what he's talking about. I know what it's like to have outsiders misunderstand a new phrase or expression. For example, me and the Grrls in my posse have some similar expressions that can be misunderstood in this same exact way. For example, if we would say "Cut the bastard's dick off!" that just means to tidy up around the house, or maybe to bake some brownies. That's all it means.

My mother loves that joke.

The few keystrokes of the computer that ended my marriage took place in a high-rise in Beverly Hills. No engraved invitations were sent, no champagne or crudités were provided. I didn't wear alençon lace or silk shantung or a veil. Because, thank God, I am not crazy. I did, however, wear a good coat of lipstick, as always.

My mother always wears lipstick; she wears it like Grrl Genius armor, and so do I. She dismissed the tepid nude tones of the seventies and the dingy browns of the eighties and stayed true to the deep, lush red she loved. My mother and I wear red lipstick to go swimming or hiking or to the grocery store or to the hospital. My mother wore red lipstick when she was giving birth to me, and I'll make sure she has a good fresh coat on before they close the lid of the coffin, or if it works out the other way, I know I can count on her to do the same for me.

When I burst into the lawyer's office, fifteen, okay, twenty minutes late, I had a moist red layer of Chanel to protect me. I also had a little smudge of crimson on the seemingly enormous chunks of enamel that are my front teeth. My husband, always the stage manager, was kind enough to point it out. After a decade of living with me, he understands that I would want to be well-groomed for my heartbreak, and I am grateful to him for that. He was very nice about my being late. I tried to make a joke, which is always the thing that saves me, but nothing I said was funny to me or anyone else.

My mother is not a person who makes jokes, though she is an excellent person to play a joke on.

My parents now live in the town on Cape Cod where I was married. For a while, they attended St. Francis, the Episcopal church that they were married in, and I was married in. After my mom's fifty summers spent on Cape Cod, the parishioners of this church, each of whom can trace his or her lineage back to the uptight Puritan freaks who populated the *Mayflower,* and who have a log the size of that great ship's mizzenmast lodged firmly up their collective ass, treated my mom like "summer people," the Cape Cod equivalent of white trash.

Although she tried to get involved in parish life, they snubbed her, and so she and my dad ended up going to the Episcopal church in Woods Hole. Despite their resignation from membership at St. Francis years ago, my mother still gets called once a year to contribute to the church bake sale. My dad works in Poland half the year, so my parents were in Warsaw when this year's insulting baked-good request came in.

As it happened, I was staying in their house and picking up their messages when I heard the impossibly pompous voice of a British woman on their voice mail.

"Hallo, this is Patty *Wilkinson* calling from St. Francis *Church.* We were *so* hoping that you would kindly bake something for this year's bake sale at the *Strawberry* Festival on June eleventh. If you can help us, we would *so* appreciate it if you would call to let us know, and then bring your baked things to the Parish Hall around nine A.M. Also, if you would be *so kind* as to please label your contributions as to whether or not they contain nuts of *any* variety. Thank you *so much,* good-bye."

I was just about to erase the message, knowing how much it would annoy my mother, when I realized that its potential for annoyance was actually the most brilliant thing about it. The call itself was supremely annoying, but how much better would it be if Patty didn't call just once, but called over and over, until she was stalking and hounding my mother with her insatiable desire for baked goods?

I launched myself into the "Patty Wilkinson Project" with unbounded enthusiasm. I spent hours perfecting the prissy, cloyingly polite voice of Patty Wilkinson, recording and rerecording myself on the phone endlessly. I managed *flawlessly* to replicate her *exact* rhythm of overemphasizing *key* words. I put in exactly the kind of time and effort and excruciating attention to detail that I never seem to put into anything involving my actual career. The all-important first message was masterful in every aspect, even down to the fact that "Patty" mispronounced my mother's first name in exactly the way that she finds the most irritating.

"Hallo, *Eeeveeey*, this is Patty *Wilkinson* calling from St. Francis *Church*. I was just calling to see if you could in fact kindly bake something for the bake sale at this year's *Strawberry* Festival. Please do give me a call at the Parish Hall if you can do that for us, and we would be *most* grateful. Thank you *so much*, good-bye."

That was on Monday. I knew my mother was picking up her messages, and I was sure that she would recognize the voice of her only daughter and call home to put the kibosh on the "Patty Project." When no call came, I was thrilled. I knew I had my mother on the hook. For the first time in our relationship, I had succeeded in annoying my mother from an entirely different continent. It was the most delicious feeling.

"Patty" called every day that week. Her calls grew increasingly frantic and obsessive.

"Hallo, *Eeveeey*, this is Patty *Wilkinson* calling once again. I have tried you a *number* of times and have received no response as to whether you will be providing any baked goods for our sale. I'm growing *most concerned* not to have heard from you, and would *so* appreciate it if you would call me at the Parish Hall to let me know either way as to whether or not you will be helping us out. Thank you *so much*, good-bye."

On Friday, "Patty" made her last, desperate, guilt-infused appeal.

"Hallo, *Eeveey*, this is Patty *Wilkinson*, just trying you one last time. I do *so* try to appreciate how busy everyone is this time of year, but I wonder if others appreciate just how *enormous* a task it is to organize the bake sale at the Strawberry Festival? I am rather *desperately* hoping that although I haven't heard from you, I will be delighted to find your contributions outside the Parish Hall by nine A.M., labeled as to whether or not they contain nuts of *any* variety. Thank you *so much*, good-bye."

Saturday morning came, and my mother had made no move to transatlantically air-express any snickerdoodles to the Parish Hall. I know, because I checked. Then "Patty" made one last, bitter, gin-soaked call.

"Hallo, *Eeveey*, it's Patty *Wilkinson*. As I'm *sure* you must know, the bake sale is now *completely over*. Apparently you have a *very* important and busy schedule to maintain. Apparently you haven't time to bake so much as *one plate of freaking brownies* for our lovely *Strawberry* Festival."

Patty, overcome with bitterness, stopped to slug back another belt of her gin and tonic, then continued, "Rest assured, *Eeveey*, that we won't be bothering you again for your help, as you are clearly *far* too important and busy to ever do something as mundane as prepare baked goods with or without nuts of *any* variety! Thank you *so much*, good-bye!"

It was then that I finally got the call from Warsaw.

Apparently it was the phrase "one plate of freaking brownies" that tipped my hand. That and how drunk Patty was.
The message from my mom began with her giggling.

"Oh, Cath, you really got me with that message. That
was just hilarious. And what's really funny is that that horrible Patty woman has been calling me all week about that
stupid bake sale! Anyway we'll talk to you soon. Bye."

Oh yes, the most indescribably delicious part of all was
that my mother truly believed that all of the *other* messages
had been real! Despite her brilliance, my mother was
apparently destined to be the ideal mark for a practical
joke. Nature helped her fulfill this destiny by having her
give birth to someone who would annoy her with these
kinds of practical jokes all her life, me.

My mother made a deal with me when I was a teenager.
If there was ever something bad for me that I didn't want to
be pressured into doing, like shooting heroin or whatever,
I could blame my lack of participation fully on her. I could
paint her out to be the most evil, vindictive harridan alive;
she was more than willing to be any kind of bad cop I
needed.

Once, when I was on a teenage date that was bad and
headed for worse, I looked at my watch, which said nine-
thirty, and pretended to go into a complete panic. I told
my thickheaded date that I had to be home by ten because
my parents were Shakers, and very strict. That Shakers were
pretty much extinct and more known for fine pegged-wood
furniture than drop-dead curfews didn't occur to my date.
He raced to get me home, apparently fearing the wrath of
my violent, pissed-off Shaker parents, whom he apparently
expected to beat him soundly about the head and arms with
meticulously handcrafted wooden spindles.

When I got home, my mom and I had a good laugh. She
asked me why I had picked Shaker. I said that it was all I
could come up with, since I was wearing a red, zippered

jacket and I didn't think Amish would fly. She, with her extensive knowledge of world religions, pointed out that I couldn't be the daughter of Shakers, because Shakers don't have sex. This was something I had forgotten, but my mom said I was probably right to assume that the boy I was out with would never have known the difference. She was thrilled to be blamed for ruining my date, as long as it kept me safe and happy.

I would love to blame my divorce on my mother, but I am pretty sure that the blame offer ran out when I hit thirty. Besides, it's not her fault. It's not really anyone's fault, it's just what happened. It's nothing to be ashamed of and nothing to be proud of.

Many years ago, when I got married at St. Francis Episcopal Church, I cried. They were tears of happiness, but you wouldn't know it from how I looked. My eyes got puffy and red, and big black rivulets of tears loaded with mascara traced their way down my face in streams as wide and soil-laden as those of the Mississippi Delta. Although I cried at my wedding, I didn't cry when I filed for divorce.

I cried later that day, in the basement parking lot of MTV, where I had foolishly scheduled a meeting to pitch a television show right after I'd filed for my divorce. I normally wouldn't schedule so much as a brow wax before a big meeting, but somehow I thought the dismantling of my heart would fit in perfectly between a business lunch and the appointment at MTV.

When I was almost at the end of my sobbing fit, my cell phone rang. It was my friend Pam T.

"Yohan! It's in Yohan!" she said, and then burst into a fit of laughter.

Even though I was red and puffy from crying, I couldn't help it, I collapsed in giggles for at least a full minute. Our hysterical laughter beamed up from our cell phones, up to a satellite circling the blue, blue earth, and then back into each other's ears.

"Are you okay?" she finally choked out.

"Yeah, I was crying in the MTV parking garage, but I'm okay now."

"Good, I just wanted to make sure. Bye! Yohan!" Pam hung up, still giggling.

The fact that I was sobbing in the MTV parking lot is not that unusual of an occurrence these days. I've been crying a lot lately. Because I am a Grrl Genius, I decided that I would use all this crying for the greater good and turn myself into a test-research subject for antipuff eye gels.

After exhaustive clinical research involving extensive hours of crying, I have discovered that Clarins *gel contour des yeux/anti-poche, anti-cernes,* is the greatest eye gel on earth. Yes, it is expensive, but there are more expensive brands. There is, however, no better antipuff eye gel in this or any other known galaxy. I am comforted to know that if I can eliminate the scarlet and swollen grief-stricken puff bags of even one Grrl Genius by recommending Clarins eye gel, my pain will not have been for nothing.

It is important to note that, although I certainly deserve it, I do not receive any endorsement fee from the Clarins corporation of Neuilly, France, for this heartfelt recommendation. However, if any employee of Clarins would like to send me some of this obscenely expensive eye gel out of the simple kindness of his or her heart, as a sort of humanitarian gesture, he or she should feel free to send it to my office at Grrl Genius World Headquarters, 6201 Sunset Boulevard #83, Hollywood, CA 90028.

My mother has no truck with eye gels or face creams of any kind. The subtle delights of smearing greasy concoctions infused with sheep jizz or snake snot or yak spittle is completely lost on her. She remains almost wrinkle-free washing her face with water only. I pray daily to my Grrl Genius higher power that, since I inherited my mother's thighs and my father's breasts, I should at least be allowed to inherit my mother's perfect complexion. Of course, only time will tell.

In my mother's family, her nickname was The Sphinx. She is wise, secretive, often silent, but always watching, listening. Our neighbor Jacquie says that with my mom's big giant brain and sphinxy ways she would have made an excellent international spy. Come to think of it, my parents have been spending a lot of time in the Eastern Bloc of Europe these days, and I suppose it's possible that my mom is, in fact, an international spy right now. It seems preposterous, but even if I asked her directly, I could never really know for sure. That's how sphinxy my mom is.

I guess that if my mother is unmasked as an international spy, I will be pretty embarrassed at the press conference.

"Didn't you think it was unusual that your mother, an ordinary housewife, spoke five languages, including Chinese?"

"Well, I don't really know—"

"Didn't you think that it was odd that she always traveled with a state-of-the-art computer?"

"I thought it was so she could write cookbooks, you know, for her church."

"Didn't the fact that she could finish the *New York Times* Sunday crossword puzzle in under an hour lead you to believe that she had extraodinary skills as a decoder?"

"It just, it just didn't occur to me..."

I love this idea of my dad's big career just being a clever ruse to hide my mom's international web of deceit. My dad, the big, blustery businessman, making all the noise and deflecting all the attention, so my mom can quietly control the fates of nations.

My mother is not demonstrative. When absolutely necessary, she will say "I love you," but she'd rather not. She'd rather sculpt your likeness in homemade marzipan or create a complex database for you. This is fine with me, because I'd rather have an accurately rendered marzipan bust or a comprehensive database any day.

I've never been all that great at giving or receiving "I love you's." Whenever people in my family talk on the phone, if someone says "I love you," that's the automatic cue to panic and hang up. "I love you" must always be immediately followed by "I love you, bye," followed by hanging up. None of us wants to hang very long after all those vast, toxic, free-floating love emotions have been released into the atmosphere, and I think that's as it should be.

I do love my mother. She is the first Grrl Genius I ever met. I love her for her class and her charm and her intelligence. I love her for loving me even though I have been a constant source of embarrassment to her. I love her for being proud of my comedy, despite that it means my getting up in front of rooms full of drunken strangers and talking about blow jobs. I love my mother so much that I have enclosed a preaddressed condolence postcard in the back of this book that you can send to my mother, extending your sympathies to her for the many embarrassing things I have discussed in this book and in nightclubs across America. I ask that you take a few moments and twenty cents to send my mother your deepest sympathy. Trust me, she deserves it.

If you send my mother a postcard, I will also send her one. It will read:

"I love you, bye."

I'm sorry, but that's the best I can do. I am, after all, my mother's daughter. Don't worry, she'll understand.

Grrl Genius Quiz Two
THE GRRL GENIUS IQ TEST

Test your Grrl Genius IQ

1. When relaxing after a hard day, I am most likely to be found:
   A. Reading the latest scientific papers on the search for the top quark.
   B. Composing a symphony.
   C. Worrying about my butt.

2. My highest creative thought is reserved for the problem of:
   A. How to create a renewable, nonpolluting source of energy.
   B. Understanding the nature of the cosmos and my relative place within it.
   C. Trying to figure out what's wrong with my butt.

3. If I had to name one Grrl Genius from history whom I could trade places with, it would be:
   A. Queen Elizabeth I, because she presided over one of the most creative periods in human history.

B. Sappho, because she was one of the most gifted poets who ever lived.

C. Audrey Hepburn, because she was a wonderful actress and she practically didn't even have a butt.

4. When I confront the most elemental questions of life, such as why are we here, and is there a God, I am most likely to answer:

A. Life is an illusion in consciousness, a temporary training ground for our souls, which are immortal and everlasting.

B. There is no external higher power; good and evil exist in the world in direct proportion to the number of sentient beings who make choices that are either good or evil.

C. If there is a God, he's probably really mad at me, otherwise, what's the deal with my butt?

GRRL GENIUS IQ SCORING:

For each A answer: 10 points

For each B answer: 15 points

For each C answer: 0 points

45–60: You're a Grrl Genius

10–45: You're a Grrl Genius

0–10: Don't you get it? You're a Grrl Genius if *you* say you are, even if you spend all day worrying about your butt!

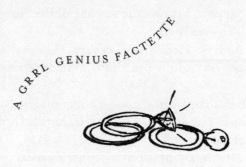

A GRRL GENIUS FACTETTE

Grrl Geniuses have superior immune systems.

Grrls get fewer colds, flus, and other viruses than men do. Scientists believe that this is because women have two X chromosomes, and it is the X chromosome that carries many of the genes that control immunity, thereby giving Grrl Geniuses a double dose. If there is a defective immunity gene on the first X, you can always go to the second X for a backup immunity gene.

So much for being "the second sex."

A GRRL GENIUS LITTLE PINK POST-IT

Hey, Grrl Genius!

What's the worst thing that anybody can call you? Obviously it's the C-word, cunt. Cunt is fighting words; call me a cunt, I'll call you dead. But what you need to know, Grrl Genius, is that the word *cunt* is actually a derivation from *Cunti,* the name of one of the most revered goddesses in the whole Hindu pantheon. This same goddess figure goes by similar names in many other cultures. In old Sweden she was Kunta; to the Romans she was Cuninia, a goddess who watched over children. The river Kent in England is named after her, and the words *cunning, ken,* and *knowledge* all derive from this same root form.

So if someone calls you a cunt, they are obviously too ignorant to know that they have called you a wise, loving, all-knowing goddess. Which you are, by the way.

A GRRL GENIUS LITTLE PINK POST-IT

Hey, Grrl Genius!

According to a recent survey, 80 percent of women "hate the way they look in store windows." Everyone knows that when you look at yourself in a store window, you usually look like you've taken an entire packet of birth-control pills and then spent all night hanging out with a bunch of deer at a salt lick. In other words, you look like you are retaining more water than the Hoover Dam.

The simple fact is, you really do look that bad, but only in store windows! It's not you, it's the windows. Almost all store windows are concave, they are slightly bowed in, which makes you look fat and horrible.

If you learn nothing more in your time on earth, at least learn this: you are a luscious, gorgeous, beautiful Grrl Genius, and store windows are an evil conspiracy in tempered glass designed to get you to buy whatever is inside the store so you won't look as awful as you did in the window.

Just say no, to store windows!

Step Twelve

Grrl Geniuses Unite

"Having Had a Grrl Genius Awakening, We Carried the Message to Others by Practicing These Principles in All Our Affairs"

Just being in a room with myself is almost more
stimulation than I can bear.

—KATE BRAVERMAN

The Jews have produced only three originative geniuses:
Christ, Spinoza, and myself.

—GERTRUDE STEIN

Neither birth nor sex forms a limit to genius.

—CHARLOTTE BRONTË

I'm so inadequate, and I love myself!

—MEG RYAN

I'll admit it, when I came up with the idea of the Grrl Genius twelve-step program, it was kind of as a joke.

Here's what I've learned: it's no joke.

Calling myself a genius on a regular basis has made my life one thousand times better. For one thing, it's made me realize how often I used to call myself an idiot. For a while, I became a sort of self-induced Tourette's victim. Whenever I put myself down, I forced myself to reflexively "put myself up." As a result, early in my program, you may have witnessed a scene like what follows.

EXTERIOR—A BEACHSIDE JOGGING PATH—DAY

Cathryn is seen roughly fondling her breasts through her T-shirt.

THE CAMERA MOVES IN CLOSER
As the camera moves in, we see that Cathryn is not in fact fondling herself, she is searching her jog bra, desperately trying to find something other than her breasts.

> CATHRYN
> (Muttering to herself)
> I'm so stupid, I'm such a moron! I can't believe I put my credit card in my bra!

Suddenly she catches herself.

> CATHRYN
> I mean, I'm a genius! I'm brilliant! Although it was certainly poor planning to put my credit card in my bra!

We slowly fade to black and Cathryn continues to palpate her breasts, hoping against hope she will find a Visa card.

END OF SCENE

How you think of yourself truly does make your world. If you think of yourself as a genius, and you say it out loud, all the time, your brain physically begins to alter. The neural pathways between the concepts of "Grrl" and "Genius" will become more easily transversed.

It is an empirical fact that you can retrain your brain. People who have had strokes or serious brain injuries learn in rehabilitation how to reconfigure their mental wiring, creating new neural pathways where none existed before. By living the Grrl Genius program, that's what you are doing, rewiring your brain, so that you can love and appreciate yourself. That is the essence of the Grrl Genius awakening.

One day, the idea that you are a Grrl Genius doesn't seem crazy or goofy anymore, it just seems true. When you value yourself, the world automatically starts to value you more.

When the (immediately imminent) Grrl Genius revolution takes place, when Grrl Geniuses rise up and begin loving and valuing their own genius, the world will undergo a paradigm shift of epic proportions. As this pink tide sweeps all the continents, all things Grrly will be seen as precious and noteworthy.

Grrl Genius solutions will become more readily accepted. Sometimes great solutions to societal ills come to me that are inspired directly from my uniquely Grrly perspective. For example, when I look at the epidemic of police brutality and corruption in Los Angeles, a massive problem that is threatening to tear this city apart, what do I, as a Grrl Genius, see?

I see nightmarishly unattractive police uniforms, made entirely of synthetic fabrics, worn in a subtropical climate. Isn't it absurd to expect compassionate behavior from individuals who are being held prisoner in poorly tailored outfits of nonbreathable fabrics? If I were forced to strut around in ass-flaw-enhancing pants of almost rubberized polyester, the screech, screech of my thighs scraping together a literal cry for help, I can't say that I might not reach for the billy club a little too quickly myself. The Christopher Commission spent millions trying to implement new rules of conduct. I say why not try implementing some nicely cut linen walking shorts with a smart, stylish flax flak jacket?

When my (upcoming) revolution is complete, brilliant, simple solutions such as these will have become commonplace. World leaders will first go have a pedicure and really think things through before they cut off diplomatic relations. Fanatical terrorists will try getting a perfect little blunt cut rather than unleashing a new reign of terror. Osama bin Laden will realize that his problems are not due to Western imperialism, but are due rather to his unfortunate taste in hats.

Fortunately, this Grrl Genius message is already being carried to the next generation. On a recent trip to Santa Barbara, my seven-year-old goddaughter, Juliet, saw a hot-pink flyer for "The Grrl Genius Club Show," a stand-up comedy benefit I do once a month with a bunch of other Grrl Geniuses and one Enlightened Male at The Improv in Hollywood, to raise money for charity.

"The Grrl Genius Club," Juliet read. She turned to me expectantly. "Can I be in the Grrl Genius Club?"

"Of course you can," I replied.

"But what if I'm not really a genius?"

I pulled her over and sat her on my lap. "Here's how it works. In the Grrl Genius Club, you are a genius because you say you are, and all your other Grrlfriends can be in your club too, as long as you're willing to say *they* are all geniuses."

Juliet scrunched up her brow the way she does when she thinks adults are being weird. "Why do we call ourselves geniuses?"

"So that we can feel confident, so that we can be proud of ourselves."

"But isn't that lying, if we aren't really geniuses?"

"Everybody in the whole world is a genius of something, as long as they are willing to be confident and figure out just exactly what it is they are a genius at. But if you're not confident, you'll never find out what kind of genius you are."

"Can boys be in the Grrl Genius Club?"

"Sure, they can be Enlightened Males. But they have to agree that all the Grrls in the club are geniuses."

"Okay." Clearly she'd had enough of the genius talk. "Do you want to watch *Gentlemen Prefer Blondes?*" Of course, there was nothing I'd rather do.

Later that week, I realized that the seeds of the program had begun to sprout in Juliet's brain. My friend Pam, her mother, went to pick her up at school. Juliet was on a far corner of the playground with a group of girls and a couple of boys.

Pam overheard her instructing the kids, "It's the Grrl Genius Club, and that means that all the Grrls in it are geniuses. Marshall and John can be the lightened males, but they have to say we're geniuses."

Oh yes, Juliet is a Grrl Genius.

She knows that she can do anything. She knows that she doesn't have to be a boy or even act like a boy to accomplish great things. It's obvious, as I watch her stand on the lawn in her gold-lamé Cinderella ball gown, vigorously chipping golf balls, that she does not think that the words *Grrl* and *Genius* are mutually exclusive.

When I was Juliet's age, I went to school and was taught to memorize the history of men, the wars they fought in, the inventions they made. I knew the president was a white man and had always been a white man. There were no women astronauts, no women on the Supreme Court.

Juliet knows that both men and women can fly in space, and since her parents are in show business, Juliet also knows that both men and women who have the right sense of style can wear gold-lamé ball gowns.

Inevitably, when I tell people about the Grrl Genius Guide to Life Twelve-Step Program, some alleged smarty-pants will point out that women are never called geniuses because most of the major artistic, scientific, literary, and cultural discoveries of the last twenty-five hundred years have been made by men.

Of course, they are correct. The assumption is that women must be big slugs and idiots, because otherwise, how come they never invent anything good?

First of all, nobody can ever say for sure who was responsible for any of the advances of the first thirty thousand years of human history. Clever little notions like the use of fire, the domestication of animals, the wheel, the planting of crops, all those adorable cave paintings, etc., are all up for grabs, since there were no good publicists at the time, and even if there were, no written language existed for them to send out press releases in.

By the time people started writing down who was inventing things, the oppression of women was off and running. For the next couple of thousand years most of the women on planet Earth couldn't have their own money, couldn't participate in the political process, couldn't get an equal education, couldn't perform sacraments in most religions. If they managed to do any of those things and stood out in any way as exceptional, they were likely to be tortured and burned alive for being "a witch." Your very life depended on avoiding being clever and interesting. Hell, you couldn't even have a best friend who was clever and interesting, because if she was clever, she was a witch, and so you were probably one too. Then you both got to become the human equivalent of s'mores.

That's quite a disincentive plan.

Wondering why Grrl Geniuses weren't making a lot of big discoveries is like wondering why death-row inmates never seem to show up at parties. Or wondering why Aborigines never seem to come up with any great software. Or wondering why slaves never seem to get good jobs.

How can you possibly win the game if you haven't even been issued the equipment?

Or as Grrl Genius Jane Austen put it:

"Men have had every advantage in telling us their own story. Education has been theirs in so much higher a degree; the pen has been in their hands."

With the (rapidly advancing) arrival of the Grrl Genius worldwide movement for world peace, economic prosperity, personal happiness, and sexual satisfaction, this will no longer be the case, and everyone will be much better off.

Because of the wild popularity of this (soon to be bestselling) book that you now hold in your hands, the Grrl Genius message will soon spread all over the world like a bad rash. In my brave new Grrl Genius world, things will be better for Enlightened Males too. Grrl Geniuses will be loving themselves in unprecedented numbers for the first time in thousands of years, and men everywhere will finally be liberated from ever again having to answer the one question that has made their lives a living hell:

"Does this make me look fat?"

Plus, all that extra, high-quality sex. (To the EM: I truly wish I had more time to go into the how and why of that phenomenon, but page length just didn't permit it. Maybe in another book, another day, but in the meantime you will just simply have to take my word for it. Sorry.)

As if I haven't given you people enough, I am going to give you my recipe for the greatest chocolate chip cookies ever made. Please see the "Grrl Genius Appendix" for the mind-blowing recipe.

Now that you are on the twelfth step of the program, carrying the Grrl Genius message to others, it's important that you know the Grrl Genius handshake. It's very simple:

THE GRRL GENIUS HANDSHAKE

When reaching your right hand out to shake, slyly wink your left eye, and touch your left index finger to your left temple twice. This handshake is recognized by declared Grrl Geniuses all over the world and is thought to be a minor facial tic by the uninitiated.

It is now time for you to also receive some of the insider Grrl Genius lingo. Just as recovering alcoholics everywhere refer to themselves as "friends of Bill W.," Grrl Geniuses and Enlightened Males refer to themselves as "friends of Cathryn M." Grrl Geniuses might also refer to themselves as a "sister of the Kreme," referring of course to Krispy Kreme doughnuts, the official snack food of the Grrl Genius program.

So. Where am I now in my gorgeous Grrl Genius life?

* Just for today, I am a Grrl Genius.

* My Graves' disease has been in remission for over ten years.

* It's been five months since my liposuction and not a single person has noticed.

* My cousin Jen, the orphan, brought her six-foot-five, tattooed, Irish, gourmet-five-star-chef boyfriend home to my parents' house and he cooked for us. He is an enormous, hulking man who will readily deliver a homily on béchamel sauce in his native Bed-Sty dialect

as he switches channels between *Monday Night Football* and the Food Channel. When he's cooking, he wears a kerchief on his head, so as he bangs around the kitchen, he looks like nothing so much as Tzeitel in the world's worst all-drag production of *Fiddler on the Roof.* His cooking is pure art, though.

The tattooed gourmet made us a five-course meal composed of exotic, ambrosial foods, most of which I'd never even heard of. The whole thing is a delicious blur, but I can recall certain highlights.

There was a cunning little oniony coulis of something with an amusing, savory reduction of something else, and apparently there was deeply musty truffle essence in that same general vicinity. This was followed by some kind of insouciantly spicy étouffée with a wry, garlicky ragout of something else entirely. Then there was an impertinently juicy stuffed fig melded with some kind of arrogantly tangy goat cheese, and I'm pretty sure there was languorously buttery lobster and velvety smooth foie gras and defiantly briny caviar involved, but to be honest I was pretty wasted from the food by then. I'm almost sure that all that was followed by some kind of a sassy chartreuse of squab with an impudently tart lingonberry confit and a witty beet puree, redolent of saffron, and possibly a petulantly crisp frisée, but not necessarily in that order.

If I had died after that meal, I would have died happy. Months after the meal, or "The Last Supper" as we kept calling it, my sister-in-law Maria and I would randomly have conversations that went something like this:

"Remember that pinky sauce?"

"The pinky sauce rocked."

"Remember how it went over the grilled things, with those little strips of that crispy stuff?"

"God, what about that crispy stuff?"

"Sometimes I dream about the crispy stuff."

"And the pinky sauce."

"No, I remember the pinky sauce, but I dream about the crispy stuff."

A few weeks ago, Jen and the chef had a big fight. My first instinct was to side with Jen, but then I remembered The Last Supper and started thinking that maybe she was being too hasty about all this. I called Maria to tell her that Jen might be breaking up with the chef.

"I can't hear this," Maria said. "This is not happening."

"I know, I know," I murmured.

"What exactly is the problem?"

"I don't know," I replied, "I mean, they're both kind of headstrong. . . ."

"Oh, please, whatever," Maria snapped back. "She has just got to work this out."

"I agree, I agree. I mean, it's not like he beats her or anything."

"Exactly. It's none of our business, but maybe we should talk to them, help them fix this thing up."

"I agree, it's none of our business, but if it doesn't clear up right away, we'll definitely have to get involved."

Fortunately Jen and the chef reconciled before we got a chance to pimp her out ourselves. I love her to pieces, and all I can say is, I really hope that she makes him happy.

* The live salad-making competition at the Santa Barbara County Fair is only eight months away and I have no idea what either my salad or my outfit will be.

* I rented an apartment by myself for the first time since I was in college. It's in the same charming little Beechwood Canyon Spanish building as my friend Marlene, who is still separated from her husband the rock star.

We have agreed that I am Mary and she is a skinny, popular Rhoda. We didn't even have to argue about it. The fact that we agreed is part of why our friendship is such a treasure to me.

* I have decided to ask the head priest at "Our Lady of the Drag Queen"—my incredibly groovy, liberal, gay Episcopalian church—to perform a small private ceremony blessing my divorce. The way I figure it, the church got me into this, so the church needs to get me out of it. The man who'll soon no longer be my husband and I agreed that we want to treat each other well in this, we want to be friends, and so I want the church to bless our divorce, to remind us to be nice to each other.

The Episcopal Church blesses lots of things. If they can bless nuclear warheads, they can certainly bless my divorce.

This is not an unreasonable request. The Episcopal Church is really the Anglican Church, the Church of England. That church was founded on the whole idea of divorce. If Henry the VIII hadn't wanted to dump his wife, there wouldn't even be an Episcopal Church.

If my priest refuses this request, I'm going all the way to the archbishop of Canterbury. If he turns me down, I'll go to the Queen of England, who is the head of the Church of England, and clearly a big fan of divorce judging by the way she treated Princess Diana.

The way I see it, these people owe me.

The Episcopal Church baptized me, and they'll bury me. They married me, and I want them to divorce me, and I won't take no for an answer.

I may also register for some gifts. The fact is, I could really use some presents right about now.

* Despite having a new place to live and having filed for divorce, the man who will soon no longer be my hus-

band has recently put forth the idea that from time to time we should still go out to dinner and then maybe have sex.

I am pretty sure that is a bad idea.

* Even though I have worked each of the twelve steps of the Grrl Genius program, there are many things about which I am completely clueless. Fortunately, as in all twelve-step programs, being a Grrl Genius is about progress, not perfection.

* My parents are back in Poland for a few months. Although they have limits on the amount of luggage they can bring, my dad refused to travel without his singing fish.

* I am now totally convinced that my mother is an international spy.

Last time she came back to the States, I watched her printing out her E-mail. She was getting hundreds of "recipes," from all over the world. Obviously, state secrets have been encrypted into these "recipes," which she then decodes and passes along to the State Department in the form of a cleverly disguised "Church Cookbook."

It's pure Genius.

* In two weeks my agent is having a "Grrl Genius Party." She is inviting twelve Grrl Geniuses, and each person is supposed to pose a dilemma to the group, and each of the Grrl Geniuses will give her genius advice on each problem. Plus there will be really good food and many festive beverages.

I encourage all Grrl Geniuses everywhere to have all sorts of Grrl Genius parties and gatherings where they celebrate and support each other's genius.

* I recently bought red plaid pants with full confidence, even though they are not in the least bit "slimming." I love them. They are cute and comfortable, and anybody who says they make me look fat can kiss my big round plaid ass.

* I woke up the other day and my very first thought was not that I am a fat, wheezing pig and a loser, but that I like me, I really, really like me.

* Krispy Kremes are excellent doughnuts.

A GRRL GENIUS LITTLE PINK POST-IT

Hey, Grrl Genius!

In no particular order, here are just a very few of the Grrl Geniuses who need to be more famous and/or adored:

Joni Mitchell, Margaret Mitchell, Maria Mitchell, Martha Graham, Martha Washington, Mary Cassatt, Mary Martin, Madeleine Albright, Louisa May Alcott, Sophia Hayden, Sophie Tucker, Tina Turner, Phyllis Diller, Dorothea Dix, Dorothy Parker, Diane Sawyer, Diana Ross, Diana Vreeland, Diane Driscoll, Diane Reverand, Rebecca West, Mae West, Sarah Bernhardt, Sandra Bernhard, Cyd Charisse, Cynthia Heimel, Cyndi Lauper, Sippie Wallace, Gigi Levangie, Samantha Dunn, Sarah Caldwell, Zoe Caldwell, Zelda Fitzgerald, Jacqueline Susann, Susan Eagan, Susan Faludi, Susan B. Anthony, Susan Stroman, Sue Murphy, Ida B. Wells, Ida Lupino, Ileen Getz, Betty Friedan, Beatrix Potter, Babe Paley, Babe Didrikson, Bonnie Raitt, Beth Littleford, Lilith, Barbra Streisand, Barbara Walters, Barbara Jordan, Julie Taymor, Jane Austen, Jane Edith Wilson, Jane Dystel, Jane Addams, Jane Wagner, Jane Curtin, Abigail Adams, Abigail Van Buren, Aretha Franklin, Laurie Anderson, Marian Anderson, Roseanne, Ann Magnuson, Ann Lamott, Maya Lin, Maya

Angelou, Marlene Passaco, Angela Lansbury, Ann Landers, Anna Devere Smith, Liz Smith, Elizabeth Beckwith, Lauryn Hill, Anita Hill, Alice Paul, Paula Poundstone, Alice Roosevelt Longworth, Simone de Beauvoir, Alex Borstein, Sacajawea, Hypatia, Boudicca, Aspasia, Anna Pavlova, Violeta Chamorro, Mileva Einstein, Gertrude Stein, Gertrude Berg, Gloria Steinem, Karen Kilgariff, Laura Kightlinger, Margaret Mead, Margaret Bourke-White, Margaret Nagle, Mellissa Banks, Marcia Wallace, Rosa Parks, Roz Chast, Robin Roberts, Janet Reno, Gypsy Rose Lee, Jean Kerr, Geraldine Ferraro, Janeane Garofalo, Julia Child, Julia Sweeney, Joy Behar, Jerrie Cobb, Judith Light, Judy Garland, Judy Tenuta, Judy Holliday, Billie Holiday, Brett Butler, Betsy Johnson, Betsy Ross, Betsy Salkind, Bette Davis, Bette Midler, Eve Arden, Eve Ensler, Eve, Isadora Duncan, Indira Gandhi, Cleopatra, Henriette Mantel, Katharine Hepburn, Catherine Littlefield Greene, Catherine de Médicis, Catherine the Great, Catherine O'Hara, Kathleen Madigan, Cathy Ladman, k.d. lang, Kathy Kinney, Kathy Griffin, Kathy Buckley, Kelly Burke, Camille Paglia, Caroline Rhea, Carol Leifer, Carole Anne Leif, Carole King, Lee Krassner, Camryn Manheim, Julia Cameron, Lena Horne, Marilyn Horne, Lea Delaria, Lillian Hellman, Lynda Barry, Linda Ellerbee, Linda Bloodworth-Thomason, Liz Tuccillo, Gracie Allen, Molly Ivins, Lily Tomlin, Nellie Bly, Nell Scovell, Patti Smith, Debbie Reynolds, Deborah Gibson, Nicole Sullivan, Teri Garr, Willa Cather, Ella Fitzgerald, Ellen DeGeneres, Ellen Cleghorne, Eleanor Roosevelt, Emily Dickinson, Erma Bombeck, Emma Thompson, Emma Willard, Emma Goldman, Judy Gold, Whoopie Goldberg, Etta May, Elvira Kurt, Edith Wharton, Kristen Johnston, Peri Gilpin, Gilda Radner, Golda Meir, Germaine Greer, Georgia O'Keeffe, Hildegaard Von Bingen, Nora Dunn, Nannerl Mozart, Natalie Cole, Minnie Pearl, Pocahontas,

Retta, Rosie O'Donnell, Rosanna Arquette, Patricia Arquette, Courteney Cox Arquette, Merrill Markoe, Sandra Tsing Loh, Margaret Cho, Sappho, Harriet Beecher Stowe, Harriet Tubman, Rita Rudner, Sara Silverman, Sabrina Matthews, Susie Bright, Sunda Croonquist, Victoria Jackson, Oprah Winfrey, Tracy Ullman, Pamela Norris, Pam Thomas, Joan of Arc, Joan Rivers, Joan Osborne, Janis Joplin, Janis Ian, Laraine Newman, Jackie Kashian, Naomi Judd, Ashley Judd, Wynonna Judd, Winnie Holtzman, Wendy Goldman, Wendy Kaminoff, Wendy Wasserstein, Wilma Rudolph, Wilma Mankiller, Stephanie Miller, Stephanie Courtney, Imogene Coca, Coco Chanel, Jennifer Coolidge, Jennifer MacClean, Chase Masterson, Rachel Carson, Carson McCullers, Carol Burnett, Clara Barton, Clara Schumann, Clara Bow, Clare Boothe Luce, Lucille Ball, Laurie Colwin, Shawn Colvin, Shawn Palovsky, Sharon Houston, Hellura Lyle, Marie Curie, Maria Bamford, Mary McCormack, Mary Queen of Scotts, Mary Magdalene, Mary Keefe O'Brien, LeMaire, Mary Tyler Moore, Valerie Harper, Fannie Farmer, Frances Farmer, Francis Fisher, Carrie Fisher, Fanny Brice, Fran Lebowitz, Frida Kahlo, Greta Garbo, Ruth Bader Ginsburg, Biblical Ruth, Sojourner Truth, the Virgin Mary, Virginia Woolf, Naomi Wolf, Billie Jean King, Queen Liliuokalani, Queen Elizabeth I, Butterfly McQueen, Empress Theadora, Lady Lovelace, Sister Wendy, Mother Jones, Mother Teresa, Moms Mabley, Grandma Moses,

And in true Grrl Genius fashion, me.

Grrl Genius Appendix #1

SEND A PREADDRESSED NOTE OF SYMPATHY TO MY MOM

Dear Evie,

Please accept my deepest sympathy on the many distasteful revelations contained in your daughter's recently published book. Her constant use of vulgarity, and her almost childish need to continually bring up embarrassing topics like her sordid sex fantasies about Howard Stern, are truly tragic.

I feel your pain,

A Concerned Reader

P.S. I thought it was particularly egregious when she insisted on discussing:

_____
_____.

I pray daily for your nightmare of embarrassment to end, but sadly suspect it will not.

TO: Evie Michon
P.O. Box 1843
North Falmouth,
MA 02556

Grrl Genius Appendix #2

PLEAD FOR THE EXPANSION
OF THE KRISPY KREME EMPIRE
THROUGHOUT THE UNITED STATES AND
ULTIMATELY THE ENTIRE WORLD

To: The (Certainly Well-Intentioned but Most Likely Extremely Overworked) Board of Directors of Krispy Kreme Doughnuts
P.O. Box 83
Winston-Salem, North Carolina 27102

Dear Sirs and Madams:

Surely you kind people are aware of the almost miraculous mood-enhancing qualities of the delectable pastries you make that proudly bear the name of Krispy Kreme.

I ask you in the name of tired, depressed, angry, lonely, and divorcing people everywhere to step up the expansion of your life-affirming pastry franchise.

Although you are already bringing salvation in the form of fried dough to countless millions of people, how much better it would be for the citizens of America if Krispy Kreme doughnuts were available, fresh, throughout the contiguous United States.

I am confident that you will take up the mantle of spreading the Krispy Kreme message of self-love throughout the land with all possible dispatch. Remember that in rapidly expanding your empire, you are not only improving the lives of ordinary people everywhere, you are truly living up to the words of that time-honored maxim of fried dough makers everywhere, "Keep Your Eye upon the Doughnut and Not upon the Hole."

Yours in Grrl Geniushood and
shared love of fine pastry,

A Concerned Reader

Grrl Genius Appendix #3

HOW TO INVEST IN THE NEW YORK PRODUCTION
OF THE BRILLIANT NEW MUSICAL
OH WELL

For further information
  please contact Sotille/Alden/Schmitz
  at their Los Angeles office:
  (323) 669-2810

Grrl Genius Appendix #4

CONTACT INFORMATION ON HOW TO BECOME A PART
OF THE GRRL GENIUS MOVEMENT WORLDWIDE

Address all inquiries to:
Grrl Genius World Headquarters
6201 Sunset Boulevard, #83
Hollywood, CA 90028

or on the Web at
www.grrlgenius.com

Grrl Genius Appendix #5

HOW THE BOOK JACKET PHOTOS WERE DONE, AND WHY NO REAL PERSON EVER LOOKS AS GOOD AS IN A REALLY EXPENSIVE PROFESSIONAL PHOTOGRAPH

From the top of my colored head to the tips of my manicured toes, not a single part of me was not in some way altered to create the image that adorns the cover of this book.

My fantastic Enlightened Male hairdresser Bill Belshya of Jonathan Salon in Hollywood puts three different artificial colors in my hair, all to create the "natural" look I covet. My hair was then loaded up with styling products and blown, curled, and teased into shape. Before the shoot I prepared my skin with a state-of-the-art facial and went to an eyebrow "expert" to have my brows professionally shaped. The artificiality doesn't end there, because I was also rigged up with false eyelashes, false nails, orthodontically straightened teeth, a padded bra, and control-top panty hose over my liposuctioned thighs. Doing the hair and makeup for each different image took at least an hour and a half. It took two all-day photo shoots, where photographers Doug Adesko and Susan Maljan spent hours setting lights and checking exposures to make sure that everything would look "natural."

To select wardrobe, I consulted two different stylists, and I was so worried about trying to create a great look that, prior to these shoots, I actually consulted with Alexis Arquette, noted L.A. drag queen, for a makeover, just to see how much is "too much." It turns out that a beaded headdress and false eyelashes that actually impede your vision are "too much."

After the pictures were taken, they were extensively airbrushed and manipulated using state-of-the-art computer retouching. Fine lines were removed, a premenstrual zit was vaporized, bra straps were erased, undereye circles were deleted. This is standard practice for any picture you see on the cover of a book or magazine. So every time you stand at the checkout counter and feel unattractive compared to the smiling faces on the magazines staring back at you, know that those smiling faces took probably a minimum of fifteen people at least a month to create.

Of course that does not include consulting the drag queen, which is optional.

Grrl Genius Appendix #6

Where to Send Complaints About This Book

Please address all complaints about this book to:

> HarperCollins Publishers
> "People Who've Never Written a Book but Think They
> Can Do a Better Job Than the People Who Killed
> Themselves to Meet Their Deadline Department"
> 10 E. 53rd St.
> New York, NY 10022

If you have written a book and have complaints,
please write to:

> HarperCollins Publishers
> "People Who *Have* Written Books but Think
> That Entitles Them to Tell Everyone Else How to
> Write Their Books Department"
> 10 E. 53rd St.
> New York, NY 10022

Grrl Genius Appendix #7

CATHRYN'S GRRL GENIUS
GREATEST CHOCOLATE CHIP COOKIES
EVER MADE

The recipe is exactly the same as that on the back of the Nestlé chocolate chip bag, *except* instead of using one teaspoon of pure vanilla extract, use one and one-half *tablespoons* of pure vanilla extract.

The resulting cookies will be one thousand times better, and no one will be able to figure out why.

Grrl Genius Appendix #8

CATHRYN'S GRRL GENIUS
CARAMEL CHOCOLATE PECAN ORGASMO SURPRISE

- - - - - - - - - - - - - - - - - - - -

1 ½ (or some) cups pecan halves

2 (or some) scoops Häagen-Dazs Dulce de Leche Ice Cream

2 (or some) tablespoons C. C. Brown's of Hollywood Hot Caramel Sauce warmed in the microwave for 30 seconds

2 (or some) tablespoons Godiva Hot Fudge Topping, warmed in the microwave for 30 seconds

whipped cream, optional

- - - - - - - - - - - - - - - - - - -

Pour the pecans over the ice cream and drizzle the warm toppings over everything. Add whipped cream, if desired.

Serves: One   Best When Eaten: Naked

Note: Go on, make it, eat it, and then try to tell me that I don't know what I am talking about.

Grrl Genius Appendix #9

CATHRYN'S GRRL GENIUS
LOW-FAT TECHNICOLOR TATER SALAD

This salad, with its garishly colorful appearance and tangy, sharp undertones, was my saladic attempt to wryly comment on the need for a new, more inclusive version of the American Dream at the Santa Barbara County Fair.

It is sure to be a showstopper at any picnic and is not impossible to make.

When you make it, you will enjoy its hearty flavor but may become overwhelmed with bitterness that so ingenious a salad remains only a third-prize winner. I can assure you that you will not be a victim of saladic ignorance, as I was, if you make this salad for your friends and family. Rest assured that your friends and family, unlike the philistine salad judges at the Santa Barbara County Fair, have no Byzantine political reasons for trying to make *you* feel "third best."

. . . .

2 (or some) boiled white potatoes

2 (or some) boiled red potatoes

2 (or some) boiled purple potatoes

2 (or some) boiled Yukon gold potatoes

2 (or some) boiled sweet potatoes

3 hard-boiled eggs

1 each red, yellow, purple, green, and orange bell peppers, diced

1 red onion, diced

1 cup low-fat mayonnaise

¼ cup nonfat yogurt

I tablespoon honey

2 tablespoons rough-cut Dijon mustard

I tablespoon sweet pickle relish

½ teaspoon paprika

I tablespoon aged balsamic vinegar

I cup diced parsley

Salt and pepper to taste

• • • • • • • • • • • • • • • • • •

Chop the potatoes and the hard-boiled eggs and put in an enormous bowl with the diced peppers and onion. In a less enormous bowl mix up all the other ingredients. Dump the less enormous bowl into the more enormous bowl and toss gaily.

Salt and pepper to taste.

Serves: Enough.

Note: Delicious if you eat it now, even better tomorrow.

Grrl Genius Appendix #10

A Dire Warning

Although I truly believe that the Grrl Genius program can revolutionize the world, I think it is important to note one of the most dangerous pitfalls that awaits those who take the leap of faith and begin working the steps. This dangerous pitfall is known as Miss America Thinking and it will knock you off the path quicker than anything else.

I realize that just the phrase "Miss America Thinking" can be viewed by some as an oxymoron, but please hear me out. Little girls all over America, whether they are interested in it or not, are aware of the Miss America Pageant. Every year in the Miss America Pageant, there is only one winner, and by default everyone else who takes part is a loser.

Everyone in the pageant must have a talent, maybe as a tap dancer or a flute player. Certainly the world needs both tap dancers and flute players, but if a tap dancer wins the title of Miss America, tap dancing becomes a winning talent, and flute playing becomes a losing talent. Miss America Thinking, imprinted on Grrls everywhere by the Miss America Pageant, can lead Grrl Geniuses into horrible, competitive, zero-sum-equation thinking, wherein a Grrl Genius mistakenly begins to believe that any Grrl who succeeds automatically becomes her enemy, the Grrl to beat. In Miss America Thinking, Grrls are prevented from mentoring each other, because there can be only one winner, and if you help another Grrl, she might beat you. Miss America Thinking feeds the delusion that another Grrl's failure is your only hope at success, and another Grrl's success is the one thing that ensures your failure.

Boys do not suffer from this delusion. They grow up watching sports contests where whole teams win, and there are so many different sports to choose from. No sport becomes *the* sport, football is no better than baseball, it's all good. Unlike in the Miss America Pageant, there is no contest where football players go up against baseball players to pick the one single most important person or sport.

Don't get me wrong, I'm not putting down the Miss America Pageant per se, although I think that there must be easier ways to get a scholarship than sliding Vaseline over your gums and epoxying a swimsuit to your butt so it doesn't crawl up your crack as you parade up and down a cruelly lit runway. By all means, enjoy the Miss America Pageant, but don't get trapped in the false ideology of Miss America Thinking.

Grrl Geniuses, you must not allow yourself to become a victim of Miss America Thinking. The world needs both flute players *and* tap dancers. Everyone's talent is unique and special, and another Grrl's success, even if you are in direct competition, does not necessarily spell out your failure.

In my opinion, nature has given women so much, they never find it necessary to use more than half.

—JANE AUSTEN
(GRRL GENIUS)

Jane had the last word for this meeting of the Grrl Genius Guide to Life Twelve-Step Program.

It Works If You Work It!

Grrl Genius Acknowledgments

Cara Hoepner, Ella Watson, Sue Watson, Gloria Swenson, Siouxzan Perry, Stephanie Miller, Faith Beth Lamont, Cara Welker, Coleen McGarr, Mrs. Nelson, Kathy Amerongen, Barbara Jane Paine Anderson, Jeanne Marie Thomas, Charlene "Luv" Jones, Sara Jane Bouchie, Renie Kramer, Jacquie Hollister, Gloria Leiberman, Jane Edith Wilson, Lori Anne Williams, Denise Steiner, Nancy Schmaedeke, Stacy Bloodworth, Nellie Diaz, Michelle Weston, Kelly Burke, Shelby Meiznick, Pam Pfeiffer, Carolyn Hanson, Keva Mosher, Margaret Meacham, Del Hunter-White, Harriet Baron, Elana Pyle, Penelope Lombard, Erin Von Schoenfeldt, Judy Brown, Debra Joy Levine, Linda Bloodworth-Thomason, Belinda Wells, Judith Light, Janeane Garofalo, Betty McClelland, Debbie Pearl, Sandra Tsing Loh, Elaine Arata, Margaret Cho, Cassandra Clark, Tracy Connor, Mirriam Goederich, Gurmukh Kaur Khalsa, Michelle Conklin, Nina Tassler, Ann Magnuson, Pat Quinn, Michelle Truffaut, Merrill Markoe, Margaret Dexter, Dee Marie Phillips, Margaret Nagle, S. Rachel Lovey, Mary Keefe O'Brien, LeMaire, Wallette, Elizabeth Karr, Robin Roberts, Jackie Kashian, Jan Bohrer, Reeta Piazza, Katherine Mason, Wendy Goldman, Winnie Holtzman, Susan Reinhart, Martha Plimpton, Carol Flint, Lydia Woodward, Sharon Hall, Ethel Mills, Denise Fraker, Lisa Lindstrom, Hayley Schorre, Sheri Kelton, Olga Truang, Tracy Trench, Maureen Donnely, Karen Taussig, Bess Walkes, Samantha Bennett, Jane Morris, Devora Moos-Hankin, Amelia David, Irene Dreyer, Beverly Case, Margaret Case, Patti

Felker, Rogers Hartman, Blanca Conches, Laurel Kitten, Mindy Kanaskie, Laina McFerren, Paige Ostrow, Mrs. Meek, Donnalee Schmaedeke, Shannon Chaikon, Laurie Steiner, Alice Cruikshank, Veronica Alweiss, Carole Bidnick, Alice Grinnell, Dottie Weiss, Ruth Juliet Norris-Clay, Carolina Jane Norris-Clay, Maya Cathryn Michon.

Enlightened Male Acknowledgments

Herb Nanas, Mr. Decker, Mr. Gray, John Wells, Bruce Watson, John Sacret Young, Bill Broyles, Phil Kellard, Rick Kellard, Tom Moore, Michael Lansbury, Mike Oggeins, Tony Themopolus, Rick Mitz, Harry Thomason, Paul Clay, Todd Glass, Rick Overton, Greg Proops, Andy Kindler, Bil Dwyer, Jimmy Pardo, Chris Pina, Dave Rath, Budd Freidman, Steve Stevens, Danny Schmitz, David Jeffry, Bill Belshya, Alexis Arquette, Andres Fernandez, Marshall Sella, Jon Hayman, Michael Halpin, Doug Adesko, Norman Stevens, Charlie Hauck, Paris Qualles, John Edwards, Dick McClelland, Joseph Anderson, David Zucker, Jim Fuller, Perry Simon, Jon Avnet, Jordon Kerner, Paul Allan Smith, Bob Broder, Joe Voce, Tom Kramer, Mark Gershenson, Tony Lawrence, Eric Vennerbeck, Ted Michon, A. E. Michon, Karl Weiss, Albert Spevak, Stu Smiley, Duncan Strauss, Michael Siskowic, Andrew Solmssen, Dom Irrera, Scott Kennedy, Mark Grinnell, Ron Fassler, Joe Purdy, Jimmy Brogan, Jay Sures, Hank Stratton, Michael Arden, Steve Trilling, Ron West, Jeff Michalski, David Zucker, Richard Aquan, Ted Weiant, Dave Bell, Bruce Blair, Chuck Martinez, John Dobson, Daniel Tosh, Steve Brown, Terry Curtis Fox, Joel Steiger, Burt Perlutsky, Matthew Fox, Keith Dion, Steve Gordon, Drew Hastings, Tom Frykman, Gary Mann, Julio Martinez, Steve Neal, Michael Marino, Bruce Smith, Richard Rorer, Matthew Guma, Arthur Giron, Garret Cohen, Steve Alden, Ross Rayburn, Gary Quinn, Michael Rayses, Paul Cruikshank, Del Close, Paul Sills, Tom Slocum, Garry Marshall, Joe Wilson, Steve Neal, Karl

Schaffer, Bud Mills, Mark Lonow, Vance Sanders, Jeremy Kramer, Blaine Kapatch, Dan Finnerty, Chris MacEwan, John Boyer, Michael Harris, Sidney Brown, Martin Schwartz, Dr. Mark Lowenstein, Dr. Michael Simmons, Dr. Soram Sing Khalsa, Dr. Allen Putterman, Dr. Raymond Massey, Les Hendrixx, John Gay, Steve Uribe, Bob Bouchie, Al Burton, Frank Conniff, Michael Bouchie, Jakob Erik Michon.

Grrl Genius Special Acknowledgments

To the greatest editor I could ever wish for, Diane Reverand, to the greatest book agent on earth, Jane Dystel, to Matthew Guma for supporting and cherishing my insanity, to Richard Rhorer and Lisa Bullaro for working so hard at making me famous, to Fred Silverman for always giving me a job exactly when I needed it most, to Chris Abbot and Norma Vela for the friendship and the jobs, both of which I needed, to Terry Norton-Wright for helping me to survive Hollywood, to Neil Stearns for "getting it," to Sat Kaur Khalsa for reminding me who I was and why I came to the party, to Saran Fox for saving my life every other day, to Barbara LaSalle for her wisdom and inspiration, to Jenny Frankfurt for the truck and all the listening, to all my precious friends in that other program, you helped me see my Genius, to Wendy Goldman for being the first member of the club, to Danny Schmitz for always taking such good care of me, to Judy Brown for telling me to be a comic, to Sandra Tsing Loh and Merrill Markoe and Ann Magnuson and Margaret Cho and Carl Reiner for being my idols and for not thinking that I suck, to fantastic Enlightened Male photographer Doug Adesko for the wonderful jcaket shot, to Suzie Skugstad and Suzanne Hidekawa for jacket design genius, to Susan Maljan for being the greatest Grrl Genius photographer of funny people ever, to Grrl Genius illustrator and world-class cat lover Kelly Burke for the amazing art in this book, to Herb Nanas for pointing out to me that I wasn't just a writer, to Gary Stockdale for being a white man with soul, to Michael

Sotille for making me go for the high notes, to everyone at Mani's Bakery for all the extra treats, to Diane Driscoll for her love and support, to Bill Belshya for being a fine hairdresser and a fine friend, to Ileen Getz and Mark Grinnell for the love, support, and Dulce de Leche ice cream, to Jen Watson for being my support system and appreciative first reader and for daring me to get that tattoo, to Pam Thomas for laughing at me on one of the worst days of my life, to the checker at Vons for carding me, to Jon Turtletaub for having a dog, to Samantha Dunn for pulling me out of deep holes and coming with me to the CAT scan, to Marlene Stevens for being the greatest friend and Rhoda I could ever wish for, to Charlene "Luv" Jones for being all love, to Judith Light for being all light, to my spiritual big brother Rick Overton for seeing only the best in me and everyone else, to Ron West for not being mad at me, to Paul Clay for being my comedian mentor and friend, to Pam Norris for being the boss of me whenever I need it most, to Duncan Strauss and Coleen McGarr for being my comedy fairy godparents, to Eric Vennerbeck for the love and the pies, to everyone at Viacom for giving me the greatest office ever, to everyone on The Stump™ for being my Jane Austen epistolary novel fantasy come to life, to Dannion Brinkley and Kathryn for fixing my writer's block, to Maria Hjelm for being the sister I always wanted, to Ted Michon for being the brother I always had and the prototype for the Enlightened Male, to my father for always telling me I was smart enough to do anything, to my mother for her love and unfathomable Genius, and finally to Eleya the wonder dog for making me stop writing and go take a walk.